HOOK ISLAND

By

Gordon Mathieson

ISBN: 978-1456329921

Cover photograph and design by Kathy Crowley

Editor: Erin Potter

Printed in the United States of America

I dedicate this book to all educators who successfully perform their daily work that parents and other citizens never see.

The education process for each child reaches far beyond the classroom.

The teachers and school administrators, who advance the academic and personal well-being of the students, exemplify what it is to be a professional.

These professionals continue to do what it takes to help the student—despite adverse challenges in the home, community, and society.

CHAPTER ONE

His silhouette stood still against the twilight sky as he witnessed the spectacular car crash. He watched in awe as the Toyota Corolla plunged over the side of Ridge Road. It tumbled over and over until meeting a wide-bodied maple tree.

The grating, bone-chilling noise of crushed metal and broken glass echoed throughout the roadside valley. The stinging maple tree branches shuddered off leaves in the wake of the violence.

Stunned at the explosive crash, the man hesitated a few moments before cautiously stepping down the steep, rocky incline. Finally reaching the base of the valley, he headed toward the smoldering crash site.

The nauseating odor of sizzling anti-freeze filled his nostrils. Stepping closer, he saw hot, steamy clouds escape from the car's buckled hood. After reaching the mangled mass, he waved his arms, dispersing the toxic clouds. He crouched down to peer through the driver's shattered window.

Early moonlight beamed into the car's interior, spotlighting the raven-haired eighteen-year-old. Still belted behind the steering wheel, her head was now grotesquely wedged between the deflated airbag and the headrest. The girl's still pose revealed a soft, smooth face of tender, youthful innocence. Her blue-green eyes, now dull and still, seemed fixed on the interior roof of the vehicle.

The horrible crash had rendered her young body lifeless, yet there were no visible scratches or cuts.

The man's outstretched arm reached into the sedan through the side window. His hand first touched the girl's sun-tanned neck. He pressed his fingers gently along the jugular vein.

Then his own heart pumped vigorously, shocked at what he felt.

Miraculously, his fingertips tingled with the soft, pulsating sensation of a heartbeat.

"Holy shit!" the man uttered out loud.

The young driver was still alive. Miraculously, she had survived the horrific crash.

Stunned with the discovery, the man reacted quickly. He stood up and pulled open the dented and damaged car door. The eerie, creaking sound echoed in the deep and dark vale. With some struggle, he managed to push the deflated airbag to one side. He reached in for the driver with both hands. In one hand he cupped the soft, smooth flesh of her chin. His other reached to the back of her head, gripping her silky, black hair.

Then with one forceful motion, his handful of hair violently slammed her head downward, cracking the girl's skull against the hardness of the steering wheel. The sudden impact snapped her slender neck, severing her spinal cord.

Taking a deep breath, the man now pressed his fingertips against her jugular vein. He once again felt for a pulse under the tender skin.

There was none.

Now, unquestionably, the pretty teenaged driver was dead.

* * *

The oppressive heat and humidity consumed every molecule of air in the second floor classroom. The restless, uncomfortable juniors reconvened at the end of the day in Room 205. They each moaned and groaned, animating their discomfort with the heavy air. Some rested their heads on the desktops, eyeing the wall clock, ready to bolt outside at the first sound of the dismissal bell.

"Okay, guys, I know we're all uncomfortable with the AC breaking down today," said Miss Lakely, sitting at her desk centered in the front of the classroom.

"Uncomfortable! This is freakin' torture, Miss Lakely. We're like prisoners locked up in a stuffy, hot cell. They shoulda dismissed us at noontime today when the system broke down!"

The comment came from a girl seated at the rear of the classroom. To cool off, she fanned a spiral notebook in front of her face which sported silver-pierced eyebrows and matching nose-ring.

The attractive teacher also fanned herself with a stiff, manila folder while forcing a smile. As she did so, a strand of her chestnut-brown hair drooped down across her forehead.

While she accelerated the hand motion in front of her moist face, she casually unfastened the second button of her white, cotton, short-sleeved blouse.

The subtle move, noticed by a few of the hormonal teen-aged boys, triggered them to gawk at the minimally exposed cleavage.

The thirty-something educator had joined the North Haven High School faculty just after the Thanksgiving break. And, the petite, perky teacher had immediately become a hit with the students and with other teachers.

Amanda Lakely had been hired to replace first-year teacher, Barry Jones, who had never returned after the autumn holiday.

Mr. Jones, the Chemistry teacher who formerly sat at the front desk in Room 205, had never been a favorite with the students. He lacked personality, and frequently talked down to the teenagers, making them feel uneasy.

The unpopular, first-year teacher also had a peculiar physical appearance, adding to his personal enigma. The social misfit tried to camouflage early baldness with gelled, platinum-blonde hair, spiked up over his enlarged skull. His pale, acne-scarred cheeks flanked a thin, protruding nose that supported outdated, purple-tinted, rimless eyeglasses.

The kids often ridiculed the strange man, making him a frequent source of unkind whispers and jokes. His students privately referred to him as "Scary Barry."

Despite being forty years of age, Jones tried to fit in with the young students by attempting to appear—cool. But his 'retro' attire made things worse. A small, diamond-stud earring pierced his left earlobe. He often wore blue jeans topped with opened-neck shirts, exposing a thick, gold chain around his neck. But his personal trademark was an oversized pinky ring worn on his left hand. The shiny band held a large, multi-faceted gemstone. The enormous zirconium stone sparkled brilliantly—diverting the students' attention during his boring science lectures.

Many of the students gossiped that Mr. Jones was a closet gay, a sexual pervert, or perhaps a deranged, mad scientist. Others wrote him off as an alien being, briefly visiting Earth from a yet undiscovered planet.

Shortly after the school year had begun last September, the principal, Mr. Pratt, held private talks with the strange, new teacher. They often met after the students left the classroom. Other times, the administrator would speak with him quietly in the hallway or in his first-floor office.

After the Thanksgiving break, Mr. Pratt announced to the classes that Miss Lakely had been recently hired to replace Mr. Jones for the remainder of the school year. There was no explanation for the teacher's sudden departure.

Today, as Miss Lakely stood up, her palms smoothed her navy-blue, pencil skirt. She nonchalantly reached for her candy-apple red cell phone. The students coveted the expensive device. It was a new model iPhone which she always kept close to her. She now lifted the cell and focused on an "app" she had just launched. After studying the text on the LCD screen, she turned and slipped the palm-sized unit into her hand bag. A rarely seen, serious expression colored her face as she addressed the students.

"Hey, listen up, gang! I just checked the local weather report online. There's a severe thunderstorm warning for this area with a chance for tornadoes. The storms are already into southern Connecticut and approaching New Haven. So, you 'walkers' had better move quickly to get home after dismissal." She stepped closer to the front row of desks as a smile returned to her pretty face.

"Just what we need to end this God-awful day!" came a response.

The teacher continued.

"Now, despite this heat and humidity, try to focus on the fact that you only have two more days of school before summer vacation! So, let's think positive, and remember, in a couple of days you'll officially become juniors at North Haven High. Congratulations! You've all survived your sophomore year!"

But today the young teacher's pep talk did nothing to change the sluggish mood of the lethargic young adults.

Amanda Lakely was different from most teachers. The teen-aged boys to men were mesmerized with her "hot" looks. The girls identified with her taste in stylish clothing. And, the students always enjoyed listening to the young educator talk of her personal stories and occasional jokes. At times her verbal and facial expressions melded with the adolescent moods and communication. She often used words like "dude," clueless," "dorky," "dope," "freakin'," and "cool" naturally, without sounding like an adult trying to speak like a teenager.

"Ah...Miss Lakely, can we, like, just kinda *sneak out* before the dismissal bell today? I mean, like, I think I'm gonna freakin' faint unless I get out of here."

The question had come from the front row of desks.

"That's not going to happen, Madison. Let's all just suck it up for a few more minutes."

"Ooooohhhhh," the young girl groaned loudly, eyes rolling upward.

The homeroom teacher then stepped closer to the rows of student desks. Still with her trademark smile, she changed topics.

"Say, I was just wondering. Are any of you signed up for the Advanced Program classes this summer? I'm just curious about who might be taking my Introduction to Logic class."

Two hands immediately shot up into the air.

Miss Lakely grinned at the nanosecond reaction before responding to the two students.

"Oh, sure, of course! I did see Becky Bing's name on the class list. I look forward to having you in class, Becky." The teacher turned to face the young male student. "And Andy, I also remember seeing your name too. Well, I think you'll both enjoy the Logic class. It's like no other course you've ever taken before. And, it should be a lot of fun! But let's hope the AC is working by then!"

Andy Abbot glanced over at Becky with a grin. She returned the smile with her own smile.

Suddenly, the soft sound of three gentle tones came over the wall-mounted speaker. The harmonic code signaled an announcement coming from the main office.

Mr. Pratt's baritone voice soon resonated over the school-wide public address system.

"This late afternoon announcement is for all faculty, staff, and students. And it's with deep regret that I must bring you this notice." There was a brief pause before the principal continued speaking.

"Sadly, I was just informed by the North Haven Police Department that one of our students died tragically last night in a car accident. I wanted to let you all know before dismissal today. The parents have already been notified. The full report will be in the TV media later this evening."

Teachers, students, custodians, administrative assistants, psychologists, and School Resource Officers all listened intently to Mr. Pratt's voice while he cleared his throat over the microphone. A pause followed with an audible sigh before he continued with his macabre announcement.

"The deceased student is one of our graduating seniors, Cindy Shea."

A short pause stalled the principal's voice.

"The police report indicated she was found alone inside of a wrecked vehicle. The car had run off of the road and hit a tree sometime last night." The muffled sound of Mr. Pratt clearing his throat interrupted his speech. "I'm sure all of you will extend your thoughts, prayers, and condolences to the Shea family. And, I'm sorry I had to give you this sad news today, but I thought it appropriate under the circumstances. More information will be provided tomorrow, including grief-counseling session schedules for those who might want that assistance."

An eerie quiet crept into Room 205 as it did throughout all of the classrooms in the four-storied building. The silence filled the empty hallways and stairwells. The shocking news combined with the heaviness in the air had subdued the students. It now seemed that the occupants had fallen into a catatonic state.

Suddenly, a shrilling cry and sobbing came from a nearby classroom. The spine-chilling sound echoed throughout the building, sending shivers to the emotionally-stunned students.

The usual, rhythmic heartbeat of the suburban high school, pulsing with high energy, had come to an abrupt halt.

CHAPTER TWO

The jarring sound of the dismissal bell jerked the students out of their emotional funk. On most days at this time, the classroom energy exploded to vacate the building, but today the students ambled out slowly, still overwhelmed with the tragic news.

Most of the teens left through the wide main doors. With book bags draped over shoulders, students headed toward the caravan of mustard-yellow buses. Others fanned out in different directions to walk to their homes in nearby neighborhoods. Once outside, the kids clustered into their usual subgroups of friends.

Andy Abbot and Becky Bing waited for their neighbor and friend, Jeremy "Bumper" Stone.

The chubby, baby-faced boy had been Andy's friend since kindergarten. But nobody ever called Jeremy by his given name. He earned the nickname, Bumper, because of his chronic habit of clumsily bumping into things accidentally in stores, in school, and inside of peoples' homes. Often these collisions would knock things down, but the mishaps never seemed to embarrass the husky young man.

Since she came from the same neighborhood, Becky joined the two boys on those days she didn't have flute, ballet, or golfing lessons.

Today, the three of them met near the school's flagpole in the center of the front lawn. Without uttering a word, the trio turned in unison, crossed

Bailey Road, and headed east toward the affluent Beechwood Knoll section of town.

They each dressed in similar fashion: short-sleeved polo shirts and washed cargo shorts to endure the heat of the season. Bumper wore his navy blue Boston Red Sox cap backwards, the visor touching the base of his neck.

As soon as they left the school grounds, Bumper pulled out a green, plastic lighter. From inside of his shorts he plucked a box of Marlboros. He flicked the lighter and lit up a cigarette.

"Man, I tell you, that just sucks about Cindy Shea!" Andy commented. "I can't believe one of our own students is now dead. I mean, I don't even know who she was, but it sucks. It's just so sad she won't be around to graduate tomorrow night with all of her friends."

"Yeah, I didn't know her either, but it does suck. I mean, she's freakin' dead at the age of eighteen! She had her whole life ahead of her," Bumper said, exhaling a cloud of toxic smoke.

Andy made a dramatic sweeping gesture with his hand to dissipate the thin, blue cloud.

"Geeze, Bump! Why the hell did you ever start smoking? You know it causes cancer, for God's sake! And if you think it's cool, it really isn't," Andy said, with an angry authority in his voice.

"Yeah, your second-hand smoke is really annoying," Becky added.

"I know, I know, but listen to this you guys! People who smoke lose their appetite and then lose weight, right? And this summer I'm gonna drop a few pounds. Hey, my aunt smokes cigarettes, and she's always been as thin as a freakin' stick! I just started, but I'll give it up as soon as I slim down a little."

"Oh, Bumper, that's just bullshit," responded Becky. "First, everyone knows smoking is as addictive as heroin and giving it up isn't very easy. And second, if you do succeed in quitting, you'll gain all the weight back. And nobody, I mean nobody appreciates inhaling second-hand smoke, for God's sake!"

Bumper ignored the sermon and took another puff, now out of spite.

The trio darted across the street toward a small public park. It was named Peck's Park after a decorated Revolutionary War hero who came from the southern Connecticut shoreline. A large wooden gazebo stood in the center of the shady treed lot. The structure was recently spruced up with a new coat of white, shiny paint in advance of the upcoming Independence Day festivities. The landscaped resting area was surrounded with tall rhododendron bushes, now boasting their vibrant, pink blooms of the season.

In single-file, the teenage trio crouched down to squeeze through a narrow opening in the tall, shiny-leafed shrubs. It led to a well-worn dirt path that served as a shortcut to the Beechwood Knoll sub-division where the three of them lived.

They felt at ease walking the hidden trail as a group, but none would consider taking the shortcut alone. The rocky dirt path meandered through a dense, ecological conservation area with wild, overgrown vegetation. The trail wound around a swampy, algae-laden, pond. It was a natural habitat for water lilies, bullfrogs, turtles, and long, black snakes.

For decades, Peck's Pond had been a favorite spot for North Haven High School teens to hang out when skipping classes or to smoke a forbidden cigarette. Younger kids would often come to the hidden pond after school or on weekends to try their hand at fishing for sunfish and perch. Many youngsters, including Andy and Bumper, caught their first "sunny" at Peck's Pond.

No words were spoken as they stepped past the shallow pond, occasionally pushing aside arching branches and overhanging wild shrubs.

Bumper's fleshy face now had streams of sweat rolling down to his chin and dripping onto his shirt. His walking pace slowed as his body felt the oppressive humidity. Becky followed closely behind, carrying her prized flute, safely stored inside its leather case. Not far behind her, the tallest of the three, Andy, took small steps as his arm swung the hard-shelled case containing his beloved, shiny chrome coronet.

The trio inhaled the sweet scents of wild flowers and tall grasses. They kept their eyes open for any rogue reptile that might suddenly cross their path. They were oblivious to the bright butterflies and bumblebees flitting from flower to flower while monitoring the threesome's journey.

At the end of the half-mile shortcut, they climbed a steep, grassy hill. Its summit bordered the rear of Smitty's Diner. As they reached the top of the incline, Bumper breathed heavily. After the climb, he labored to catch his breath then turned his crimson face toward his two friends.

"Hey! You guys stoppin' in for a cold drink? I could sure use one today with this freaking heat!"

"Yeah, sure. I'm kinda thirsty," replied Becky.

"Yeah, that's cool," Andy said as a loud, rolling rumble of thunder echoed in the distance.

For many years, Smitty's luncheonette had been a popular gathering place for Beechwood Knoll residents both young and old. One side of the diner had an old-fashioned soda fountain setup with a polished, marble counter top. The swirling counter stools were a favorite for kids of all ages. Other patrons preferred sitting in the bright red, tufted oil-cloth booths.

Today, the three friends chose an empty booth inside the comfortably air-conditioned restaurant.

A middle-aged, uniformed waitress appeared just as Andy carefully set his coronet case on the bench-styled seat. Becky and Bumper slid in on the opposite side of the table facing him.

Andy ordered a Cherry Coke; Becky, a Diet Sprite, and Bumper, a Mountain Dew.

"Hey, guys, I think we should get a small pizza," Bumper suggested. "Whatdya' say? It'll be my treat!"

As Bumper gave his pepperoni and cheese order to the waitress, Andy glanced over and winked at Becky. It was an unspoken message about their overweight friend's typical eating habits.

Later, while sipping their cold drinks, they talked about the beginning of summer vacation coming up and what they each wanted to do with the time off. The discussion then segued into the horrible car accident that took Cindy Shea's life. The three of them agreed they would attend any scheduled memorial services together.

While their heated bodies became comfortably cooled inside the air conditioned restaurant, a sudden, heavy downpour of large raindrops followed a loud rumble of thunder. The splashing noise of rushing water briefly interrupted their conversation while they peered outside the restaurant window.

Bumper leaned into the table and whispered to his two friends.

"Hey guys, I want to let ya' know something I just learned last night. It has to do with a cool, one-night, concert gig. And it's something that'll happen not far from right here. *But it's wicked, top-secret. Once I tell you this, you can't tell anyone!*"

Andy gulped a mouthful of the soda followed with a loud swallow that oscillated his Adam's apple.

"What the hell are you talking about, Bumper? What's this, this *wicked, top sec*ret about a one-night gig? Are the *Rolling Stones* coming to our little town for a one-night concert?"

Becky giggled at the ridiculous question.

"No, no nothing like that oldies celebrity crap. But what I have to tell you is gonna happen. And, it's gonna happen right here in Beechwood Knoll!"

"Okay, okay, Bump, so give it up. What the hell is it?" Becky asked impatiently. She anticipated hearing some gossip that her chubby friend had just picked up.

Bumper's eyes swiveled, panning the luncheonette in dramatic fashion. It was obvious he was making sure nobody was within earshot. He then leaned into the table once again and spoke in a soft tone, almost whispering.

"Do you guys remember that cool rock band, New Age? They came from New Haven but broke up about two years ago. I guess they had some money issues and split up but this happened after they made some really cool tunes. Man, when they were at their peak they sold a ton of CDs. You know, for a while they were the number one group on iTunes lists. They also had an awesome video that played on MTV!"

"Yeah, yeah, so what? Is that the *secret*, Bumper?" Andy asked.

"No, no. Listen to me! The lead singer, Jimmy Angel, is bringing the group back together. And— they've been secretly jamming each night getting ready for a major comeback."

"So...so, what the hell's that got to do with Beechwood Knoll here in North Haven? Besides, that rock group came from New Haven. And I wouldn't call them getting back together for an attempted comeback some wicked, top secret information!"

Bumper once again slowly peered around the near-empty restaurant, creating some mystery to his unfolding story. His voice was just above a whisper.

"Listen, you guys, this really has to be kept under wraps. My cousin, Frankie, is now working as one of the sound crew with New Age. He told me the group is secretly practicing over at the old, abandoned Hook Island factories. Nobody knows about it. It's a great place to practice because nobody ever goes out there to that God-forsaken island. And, it's away from everything so nobody hears them."

"Hmm, sounds like a good choice for something like that," Becky commented.

"Yeah, and Frankie told me a few of those old, abandoned, factory buildings still have electricity to keep the sump pumps running. So, the band jams out there, getting the group into shape while out of sight. And, the best part is...Frankie invited me to join him *tonight* to watch them!"

The waitress brought the steaming pizza to the table. Each of them quickly peeled away a piece of the hot pie, raising it up in the air. They took turns ceremoniously stretching out strings of gooey mozzarella cheese.

"OK, so that's cool, Bump. You get to see a private rehearsal session of the New Age jamming tonight. Sounds like you're gonna have fun!"

"Yeah, well, especially tonight because this is their last practice before they go public. My cousin is gonna travel with them on their road trips. New Age has a new concert tour they'll announce soon. It'll start at Toad's Place in New Haven. Then it's off to Hartford and on to Boston later this summer."

"Sounds like a good time to me! And, a nice way to spend one of our last nights of the school year," Becky said before devouring a bite of pizza.

"Hey, why don't you take some video of the group, Bumper?" Andy suggested. "It'd be so cool to own a one-of-a-kind 'vid' of the band during one of their secret practice sessions."

"Yeah, well, that *was* my plan, too. I thought it'd be awesome to own something that nobody else has. And when New Age makes their big comeback, that vid will all of a sudden become so freakin' valuable! And ya know, I wouldn't even put it on YouTube or any other websites for free. I'd make some quick cash out of it, like selling it on EBay or Craig's List or something like that!"

"Hell, yeah! I think that's a great idea!" Andy said, gnawing on a crispy pizza crust.

"Yeah, but see, guys...I got a problem doin' that. Frankie told me taking *any pictures* at the old factory building was strictly taboo. The secret practice sessions are still unknown to anyone except the crew, a few friends—and now me. And they want to keep it that way."

"Oh...that sucks," Becky said, wiping her long, slender fingers with the white paper napkin. "But at least you get to see and hear them play some of their tunes tonight."

There was a long pause before Bumper spoke again. He dropped his head down then raised it slowly to look at his two friends.

"Yeah, it does suck that *I* can't take a video, but, but—*you two guys can do it.*"

CHAPTER THREE

With a puzzled expression, Becky looked across to her friend, Andy. She noticed his left eyebrow arched with curiosity before he responded.

"*We* can do it? Bump, *how the hell can we take a vid of New Age*? We aren't even invited. And they don't want any publicity about where their band is practicing before their comeback tour. You just freakin' told us that!" Andy shouted.

"Shh! Keep it down for God's sake!" Bumper hissed. Then in a soft whisper he continued. "I didn't say *you'd be invited.* But I have an idea. If I tell you exactly where the band is jamming, you know like, inside of which factory building, you two could take some hidden video without anyone knowing you're doing it. Think about it!" Bumper's tone escalated with enthusiasm. "You guys could tape the whole fuckin' thing! And the band would never know they were bein' filmed."

"Hidden video? Hidden video?" Becky said, mimicking Bumper's soft whisper. "What…what the hell are you talking about?"

"Look, we've all crossed over the Hook Island Bridge to those old, empty island factories many times. Hell, Andy, you and I used to ride our bikes over there every day when we were little kids. We used to snoop around and play hide and seek around those creepy factory buildings."

"Yeah. So what?" Andy asked.

"So, I know exactly which building they'll be in tonight. Now, check this out. I'll already be inside the factory, but if you guys stay hidden outside by one of those broken windows, you could film the whole thing. And, you'd get to listen to some cool music at the same time!"

"Tonight?" Becky asked.

"Yeah, I just told you this was their *last night* jammin' on the island. That's why my cousin is bringing me along. C'mon, Becky, keep up, will ya?"

The impatient sarcasm didn't go unnoticed.

"Geez, Bumper, I don't know. Sneaking pictures of the rock group sounds freakin' weird and perhaps—criminal," responded the petite young girl as she took her last sip of Sprite. "You know, we'd be infringing on their rights to privacy."

"Oh, Becky, you're always so...so practical, always so...so fuckin' law abiding. Why don't you just loosen up for once and enjoy some excitement in your life? You know, be adventurous!"

"But hell, Bump, I have to agree with Becky. I don't think this is so...so, exciting. I mean, I like most kinds of music, but I was never a big fan of the New Age. I mean, granted they sold a lot of CDs back when, but they didn't last very long with all of their other—*issues*. So what's the big deal for us?"

Becky's cell suddenly beeped with a text message alert. She pulled it out of the front pocket of her khaki shorts.

"Yeah, I agree. I was never a big fan of the New Age band either," Becky said, looking down at her cell and texting a return message with the tips of her thumbs.

Bumper didn't try to hide his disappointment as he stared at each of them.

"You know, it's just like you guys to wimp out on me. And it really, really pisses me off! I think as your long-time friend, Andy, you could do this one simple favor for me. I can remember helping you out of a few scrapes in the past. And I never asked you to do anything for me. I guess you think my plan is some freakin' stupid idea. Or is it because you two are in those nerdy, advanced classes together, and I'm down with the idiots in the lower levels?"

Andy recalled the particular incident his friend had just referenced, although it had happened years ago. It was back in the fifth grade at Beechwood Knoll Elementary School.

At that time, a very slight Andy Abbot had been tormented by a heavyweight bully every day in the school. Outside of the building, the bully often beat Andy and called him names such as "Candy Andy."

When Bumper found out about his smaller friend's dilemma, he called upon some of his oversized classmates. One afternoon there was a showdown behind the school. It was totally one-sided and the bully immediately backed down, never to intimidate Andy Abbot again.

Today, Bumper was calling in his chip from that day long ago behind the elementary school.

Becky sensed the awkward situation for Andy. She reacted by proposing a solution to defuse the tension. She lowered her voice to a near whisper.

"I tell you what, Bump. I'll go out to the factory if Andy goes, but I can't stay long. I need to be home before nine, because it's still a school night. I'll tell my parents I'm going out to visit a girlfriend but won't mention going over to the island. My folks would have a conniption if they knew I went to Hook Island at any time, but they'd really freak out if they knew I went out there at night."

Andy picked up on her compassionate support and jumped on his cue to agree with the plan.

"Yeah, okay, Bump. You can count on me, too. But if New Age plays late into the night, I gotta get my butt home too so my mom and dad don't worry."

Bumper's face beamed with renewed excitement and manipulative victory.

"Sure, sure, of course! Hey, this is great, guys! Andy, you gotta bring your new camcorder you just got for your birthday. And you both gotta be there by eight o'clock, okay? Now, the session's gonna be held in Building C1 at the far end of the island. The group will be setting up around seven-thirty."

He looked at the serious expressions on Becky's and Andy's faces.

"Hey, c'mon guys, this will be great! This gig is all dope man! It'll be cool!"

After Bumper paid the check, the trio left Smitty's Diner. They became quiet once again as they walked along the rain-soaked sidewalk. Their minds were consumed with anxiety about their secret mission out to Hook Island scheduled for later that night.

* * *

At seven-fifteen that evening, Andy sat on his bike watching Becky cruise towards him on her own ten speed Trek bike. She stopped when she reached the corner of Bridge Road. They both felt the heaviness of the humid, cloudy evening with the imminent threat of more rain in the air.

"Did you remember to bring your camcorder?" Becky asked after pulling out her iPod ear buds.

Without a word, Andy pointed to his saddle bag tucked behind his bicycle seat.

They briefly stared at one another. Then, as if on cue, they each took in a deep breath and exhaled feeling the anticipation of the night. They spun off, and headed toward the shoreline island.

Becky wore a swept back, electric-blue biker's helmet. Andy had on his dark maroon headgear with the popular Nike logo on either side.

After they pedaled for nearly five minutes, the paved road ended, interfacing with the old, weathered, wood-planked bridge. The aged structure crossed over a stretch of marshland and a wide, salt water estuary that originated in Long Island Sound. The body of water had always been referred to as "Hook River." It penetrated the land in a serpentine way along the fringes of southern Connecticut, ultimately terminating in the marshy shoreline of North Haven.

Tonight, the estuary's streaming current moved swiftly with the evening high tide approaching. The hundred-year-old, rusty, iron-framed bridge supported many wagons and trucks that had crossed each day during the height of the Industrial Revolution and decades after. The vehicles had carried a payload of raw textile material to be spun into a variety of fine cloth material. During its peak operation, small cargo boats would sail into the waterside of Hook Island docks and pick up the finished products. They would then transport the goods to large freighters anchored in Long Island Sound destined for further shipment around the world.

The island had always been considered a geological marvel. Unlike other glacier deposits on Long Island Sound, the mile long underbelly of Hook Island was made up of thick, impervious limestone. Its depth and density was ideal for excavation and to support structures to be built with only minimal risk of seawater penetration.

After the two teens pedaled over to the other side of the bridge, the large metal sign, now rusted, caught their attention. They both read the warning which sent a slight chill down their spines. Breaking the law, any law, was not in their usual repertoire.

**PROPERTY OF HOOK ISLAND TEXTILES
ABSOLUTELY NO TRESPASSING!
VIOLATERS WILL BE PROSCECUTED**

Something else caught their attention as they cruised by the sign. A solitary man was walking off of the island in the opposite direction of their pedaling.

Surprised at seeing someone else on the property, they continued pedaling, looking straight ahead but glancing obliquely at the lone pedestrian.

The thirty-something man wore a tight fitting, black muscle t-shirt and straight blue jeans. His long, black hair nearly reached his shoulders. His chest was broad, topping a flat, six-pack stomach. A tiny, gold hoop earring hung from his left earlobe. But it was his arms that were so imposing with biceps cut like those of a professional body-builder. His forearms were completely covered with intricate, abstract tattoos of red, green, blue, and yellow ink. The man held a cell phone to his ear as he paced. He walked by the two young bicyclists without as much as a nod. But his conversation could be overheard by the passing teens.

"Hell, I don't know what's going on inside there!" he said, with anger. "There's some kind of rock band setting up to practice."

A short pause followed.

"Huh? How the hell would I know? I guess maybe a dozen or so counting their damned groupies. And right now there are a couple of young kids biking over that way. What the hell's going on here tonight, a damn concert?"

The teens cruised past the man, out of earshot of the rest of his conversation. They continued on the bumpy and crumbled pavement that led to the old, abandoned factory buildings.

"So much for Bumper's top secret jamming session tonight," Andy yelled over to Becky, as they slowed their bikes. "We aren't the only ones here tonight besides the band and the crew."

"Yeah, for all we know that guy was probably talking to the press. I bet it'll be on the front page of the New Haven *Register* tomorrow morning," Becky replied with a grin.

The first row of dilapidated factory structures showed no life, nor did the second set of run-down, weathered remnants. But as the two cruised toward the furthest structure, Building C1, they spotted a few vehicles parked close by.

Low, thick clouds blocked any moonbeams on this evening, making it darker and seeming later than it was. The teenagers pulled up to the old, defunct factory, stopping nearly twenty yards away. Andy spotted a narrow alleyway about a meter wide between the two adjacent buildings. He looked around and then walked his bike toward the opening. He quietly motioned for Becky to follow him. The dark, tight passageway was a perfect spot to hide their bicycles and helmets.

Andy opened his bike saddlebag and pulled out his parents' recent birthday gift to him—a new, Sony digital camcorder.

Suddenly, a blaring sound bellowed from inside the factory as the saxophonist tuned up. This was followed with an unpleasant mix of sounds, as musicians simultaneously tested their instruments. Walking carefully to the side of the building, they spotted a window already opened.

"Look! They must have opened it up already to get some air. We can use it to get a good view," Becky whispered, showing no signs of nervousness.

The two stooped down, sneaking along the weathered brick foundation wall until reaching the window. It had been flipped open and held with a rusty-brown eye-hook.

Becky and Andy slowly stood up from their crouching position until their eyes could peek over the weathered window frame.

The lighting wasn't perfect but they could peer down onto the former factory machine operations room on the lower underground level.

Four performers made up the New Age band. The popular lead singer, Jimmy Angel, was the icon for the group and seemed to give direction to the others. There were standing microphones set up with large speakers surrounding the makeshift stage area. A thin, pony-tailed man standing behind the keyboard motioned for everyone to get ready.

As the musicians started their first number, Andy panned around with his camcorder held out at arm's length. The moving camera found others in the room besides the band members.

The groupies sat about twenty yards away from the band, some sitting in beach-type folding chairs, and others on the factory floor. They all moved in time with the music, encouraging the band. The audience, all women, sat drinking from beer bottles or soda cans. Some were smoking cigarettes of the legal kind, while others used a different weed. The band members and sound crew appeared to be in their late twenties or early thirties.

While Andy focused his camera on the band members, he also panned around the audience looking for Bumper. But their chubby friend was nowhere in sight.

Andy continued recording the video after the group finished playing their first tune and then picked up with the rest of the set. The loud music echoed from the jumbo speakers throughout the emptied factory floor. His camera panned over every inch of the factory area, focusing on the band and then zooming across to the enthusiastic audience.

Suddenly, a vibration coming from Andy's pocket indicated an incoming text message. He pulled out his BlackBerry, checked the lit up screen, and then whispered to Becky.

"Hey, it's from Bumper. Here, you take the video."

He handed the camcorder over to Becky so he could read the incoming text message.

Becky continued to record the images and the sounds coming from the lower level of Building C1.

After a few moments, Andy leaned into Becky while putting away his BlackBerry. He whispered into her ear, "Bumper just texted me that he won't be here tonight. He had a family emergency and had to go into New York City with his mom."

Without responding, Becky handed the camera back to Andy. They'd complete their mission as they had agreed for their now absentee friend.

Just as Andy resumed his position leaning on the window sill, he and Becky heard the whirring sound of a car engine approaching.

But it wasn't just one car they heard. There were several. Their heads swiveled around to look behind them. Bright, white headlamps and flashing red and blue strobe lights atop police cruisers were speeding directly toward Building C1.

CHAPTER FOUR

Three North Haven Police cruisers rolled across Hook Bridge, approaching the defunct factories. Although the strobe lights lit up the murky sky, the sirens were silent.

The vehicles turned directly toward the spot where the teenage stalkers crouched by the opened window at Building C1. One car stayed back by the old wooden bridge.

Becky and Andy froze in place—their eyes opened wide but unable to move a muscle as they stared at the short parade of cop cars coming towards them.

But as the blue and white cars approached, they suddenly spun off toward the rear side of the building. Andy didn't move from his hunkered position. His hand gripped the camcorder resting on top of the window sill.

Becky's eyes swiveled back and forth then stared at him without her body moving a muscle.

"Look, Andy, there's still one cruiser hanging back. It's blocking the bridge so nobody can escape this…this raid." She spoke in a soft, nervous whisper.

Suddenly, a man's loud voice bellowed through an electronic bull-horn.

"THIS IS THE NORTH HAVEN POLICE! I WANT EVERYONE INSIDE THE BUILDING TO GIVE ME YOUR ATTENTION!"

The sudden, squawking noise jolted Andy's tense body, causing him to lose grip of his brand new camcorder. The device slipped out of his hand, quickly tumbling down toward the factory floor.

"Oh, shit! There goes my camcorder," Andy whispered.

Both he and Becky reacted, poking their heads inside the window opening. Their mouths opened wide as they caught sight of the shiny camera turning end over end. Their eyes followed the descent until it landed on a high pile of old textile materials. Fortunately, the impact was soft and noiseless, bringing no attention from the already stunned rock band and audience.

As the two friends peered downward, they could barely make out the tiny red LED. It was still lit— indicating the camera was still on and silently recording.

Becky spoke softly, "We can't get it now."

"Okay, okay. I know. We'll just have to leave it down there for now. Follow me. Let's hide by our bikes in the alley."

Becky nodded and followed behind Andy. They both crouched low and awkwardly waddled toward the darkened alleyway. As they did so, large rain drops began to fall.

"THIS IS THE NORTH HAVEN POLICE! WE'RE COMING INTO THE BUILDING. DO NOT PANIC. WE WANT ALL OF YOU TO LAY FACE DOWN ON THE FLOOR WITH YOUR ARMS AND LEGS OUTSTRETCHED. WE HAVE THE BUILDING SURROUNDED AND THE BRIDGE IS BLOCKADED. PLEASE COOPERATE AND NOBODY WILL GET HURT!"

The cop spoke with unwavering authority in his loud, commanding voice.

Suddenly, the unmistakable noise of the police cruiser doors opening and slamming closed made Andy's body flinch once again.

Nervous thoughts raced through his head as he anticipated a bad ending to the night's trip out to Hook Island. With the darkness of the night and a drizzly rain now falling, he could barely make out Becky's petite silhouette stooping next to him.

The sheet of misty rain reflected the police car's bright strobe lights in the distance. The vehicle was parked sideways to block anyone from crossing over the old wooden bridge. It was certain nobody would escape Hook Island tonight until the police allowed it.

Without warning, a narrow, bright beam from a hand-held flashlight swirled around on the ground near the alleyway. The two teens squeezed closer together and closer to the damp ground. When they looked up they could see two uniformed cops patrolling on foot around the building. Their vigilant patrol would ensure nobody had already escaped the factory building.

Andy's body trembled as he peeked out from the darkened alley. Watching the swirling beams of light come closer to the alleyway, he swallowed hard with an audible and nervous gulp. Becky heard the sound.

As they hunkered down in the misty blackness, a hand reached out from behind Andy and then grabbed and squeezed his bare arm. His heart stopped. The unexpected contact on his damp flesh alarmed him, raising the hair on his arm. Now the fear froze him in place. He was afraid to turn and face an angry cop.

When he finally turned in the ink-like darkness, he realized it wasn't a cop's hand who had gripped his arm, but Becky's. Her soft fingers now slid down to his hand and held it firmly in her own.

Becky could feel the tingling nerves inside of Andy's flesh. She gently squeezed his hand to reassure him that they'd both be all right. She leaned into him and whispered her plan softly into his ear.

"We'll wait 'til the cops walk by once more on their way back—then we'll make a run to the edge of Hook River."

"What...what about our bikes?" he whispered with a dry voice.

Before Becky answered, Andy sensed her lips brushing against his ear. He could feel her warm breath on his earlobe.

She continued to whisper.

"Don't worry! We'll come back for the damn bikes tomorrow. Besides, there's no way we can get by the bridge blockade. We've got to get our butts out of here soon or we'll be arrested by the cops for trespassing and God knows what else!"

She gradually loosened her grip on his hand.

"Okay," Andy said while nodding his head, trying to hide his raw and rattled nerves. But what he heard next froze his whole being and stopped his heart pumping.

The sound of men's footsteps could be heard along the crumbling asphalt. And the steps were once again coming closer to the hidden alleyway. Then a bright beam of light danced upon the ground, not far away from the two teens.

The pair of cops swept their beaming flashlights back and forth as they came closer. Becky and Andy squeezed closer, leaning against their bikes to avoid the sweeping beam of light. Then the unexpected happened.

Crack!

The sudden sound and explosion of light seemed to pierce through every nerve in their young bodies.

A brilliant bolt of lightning had struck close by, illuminating all of Hook Island as it streaked across the dark, cloudy sky. The brilliant flash made everything appear clear in a wash of light blue.

This was immediately followed with a ground-shaking roll of thunder.

The two teens catapulted up from their crouched position, startled from the roaring sound and earth-shaking vibration.

The thunder heralded a torrential downpour that splashed down upon the decayed asphalt factory lot. The rain was so heavy it produced a grey, wet veil against the black sky, reducing visibility to just a few feet.

"Holy shit! This is a helluva monsoon, Bill. Make a run for it!" a patrolman yelled out.

His partner responded. "Yeah, let's get our butts back into the cruiser!"

The uniformed men's footsteps splashed through puddles as they ran past the alleyway toward their police car. Soon the sound of car doors slamming closed confirmed they were a distance away.

"Okay, Andy. We gotta make a run for it. Now, let's go!" Becky commanded in a voice just loud enough to be heard above the pounding rainfall.

The duo bolted from the alley as fast as their young legs could carry them. They sped in the opposite direction of the bridge. Hidden by the heavy, pouring rain and dark of night, they continued to run into the marshy banks of Hook River. When they finally stopped at the water's edge, their nervous and labored breathing was now louder than the sound of the pounding raindrops. They peered up toward the bridge guarded by the police cruiser some distance away. A rotating spotlight affixed to the police cruiser scanned the area in wide circles, forcing the teens to hide behind a utility pole.

Becky now stood very close to Andy trying to catch her breath. His tall, slender stature overshadowed her petite figure. She glanced up and stared at him to check that he was all right. The rain had flattened down his thick, chestnut-brown hair, giving him a distinct single part down the middle of his skull. Soaked and separated clumps of bangs stuck to his forehead.

While the thunder rumbled and the lightning continued to flash, Becky grinned at her friend's silly appearance. But she realized she probably looked just as comical, or worse. She sensed her pointed, pixie-like ears now protruded out with her soaked, black hair swept back and dripping down her neck.

"Hey, Beck, I just thought of something. Can you swim?" Andy asked, still catching his breath.

"Of course I can! What the hell do you think—that I don't know how to swim?" Becky retorted defensively.

With the raindrops still pounding loudly on the ground, they ran closer to the estuary. Without hesitating or looking behind them, they took a deep breath and simultaneously dove down into the salty seawater. Already drenched to the skin, there was little physical shock from the chilled water on their bodies. They immediately began swimming across the raging current.

As arms stroked frantically and legs splashed in the choppy water, loud thunder and bright veins of lightning provided a frightening background.

Becky soon outpaced her tall friend with her smooth strokes and trained kicking. At each lift of her arm, she peered back at Andy. With the sky lighting up every few seconds she caught a glimpse of the helpless fear on his face.

Becky had no difficulty cutting through the rapidly churning water, but she kept a watchful eye on the struggling Andy. She then purposely dropped back several yards to swim parallel with him. Her physical closeness provided a sense of security and gave him a burst of needed encouragement.

Finally, the two reached the bank on the opposite side of the estuary. They slowly pulled themselves up onto the soggy *terra firma*. Still reeling from the challenging swim, their legs felt weak. By this time they were both oblivious to the heavy rainfall. As they wobbled up onto the marshy vegetation, their soaked athletic shoes got sucked into the soft, wet muck. Completely drenched, they weaved in and out between tall, cat o'nine tail plants and sharp-edged sea grass. Slogging their own pathway through the mushy marshland, they finally reached the abutting road and welcoming streetlights of Beechwood Knoll.

As soon as they stepped away from the soggy marsh area and onto the puddle-filled, paved street, the rain slowed and then finally ceased. Now the rolls of thunder could only be heard off in the distance. Within minutes, the summer moths came out, fluttering white wings toward the brightness of the street lights.

The nasty storm had completely passed.

The duo walked side-by-side without saying a word, down the middle of the street. Each step was accompanied by a loud, squishing sound, mud squirting from their waterlogged athletic shoes. The damp scent of rain-soaked asphalt filled their nostrils as they ambled along the vacant street.

They remained silent while still recovering their normal breathing rate. It gave them time to digest what they had just experienced. Tonight's frightening episode was unlike anything the two honor roll students had ever imagined might happen to them.

Becky finally broke the silence. She decided to talk about something not related to their daring escape.

"So, Andy, you never told me. What the hell's wrong with our good buddy, Bumper? What was his so-called emergency in New York that he couldn't be there tonight?" Becky asked.

They both stared straight ahead as they walked toward their neighborhoods. "Oh, his text message only said he had to leave town with his mom. His grandfather is very sick and it didn't look too good. His mother wanted to be there, and since Bumper's dad is out of the picture, he went with her."

"Hmm, that's too bad. And...he'll be pissed that he missed all the freakin' excitement tonight. Especially, since it was his grandiose plan to get a vid of his favorite band on Hook Island."

They both chuckled at the irony.

"Yeah, but I'm just happy we escaped the real excitement! I didn't want to get pulled down to the police station and have to call my parents. And, why do you think there were so many cops there to make the bust, Becky? I mean, geez, I would've thought one cruiser could have done the job."

"Yeah, I know what you mean. But right now I don't have a clue. I'm sure we'll read about it tomorrow in the *Register*."

They finally arrived at the corner of Becky's street and stopped walking. Each turned to face one another under the soft light of the streetlamp. After a deep breath, Andy looked straight into Becky's eyes before speaking.

"Okay. So, we cleverly escaped arrest by the North Haven cops tonight without any trouble but what do you think we should do about..."

The tall teen stopped speaking mid-sentence.

He had lost his train of thought and completely forgot what he was going to say. Instead, his eyes remained locked onto Becky's face as she looked up at him in the dim light. He couldn't seem to get out any more words, nor did he care. He was mesmerized by what he saw.

Was Becky Bing always this hot-looking?

The young man noticed for the first time how his friend had the cutest dimples when she smiled. After all of the classes, all of the band practices and school events they had shared for the past two years, he now saw his close friend in a completely different way.

But it wasn't just the visual image that struck him unexpectedly. Now there was a stronger bond between them. He now knew that Becky cared for him. She proved that in the Hook River current tonight when she drifted back to swim beside him. She knew he was struggling across the raging river during the storm. He didn't think he'd make it across safely. But she knew he was in trouble and stayed by his side to encourage him. And she did it without saying a word.

Something else was happening now that he had never experienced before. Still without speaking, his eyes peered directly into the inviting eyes of the shorter, black-haired girl looking up at him.

Her golden-toned face seemed to glow tonight as she stood facing him. Her dimples deepened into a broader smile as he stood staring at her.

"Hey, Earth to Andy, Earth to Andy. Are you there? Snap out of it! You never finished asking me your question. Are you having a 'brain freeze' or something?"

Andy shuddered as he came back to reality.

"I, ah…ah, I was just thinking, Beck. I'm gonna still have to go back to Hook Island tomorrow night to get my camcorder that dropped inside the factory. Will you, will you, ah….do you wanna go back out there with me?"

But Becky didn't answer him. Instead, and without a word, she stepped closer to him. She slowly raised herself up on her tiptoes. Then she casually raised her arm up toward Andy's face, moving her hand close to his still dampened cheek.

Andy then felt the gentle touch of her fingertips on his face. His heart pumped rapidly inside his chest. He didn't know what she was doing but he kept his eyes locked onto hers. The light touch of her fingernails on his face sent a tingling sensation throughout his whole body.

"I don't think you want to show up at home with this on your cheek," Becky smiled.

"Huh?"

Her fingers gently peeled off a small piece of emerald-green seaweed from the side of his face. She dangled the algae in front of his eyes.

"Huh? Oh yeah. I mean, ah…no, of course. Thanks."

She then turned to walk down the street to where she lived.

"Okay, Andy!" she yelled out, in the dark night without turning back to face him.

"Huh? What? What's okay?" he shouted back to her.

"Okay! Okay! I'll go back to Hook Island with you," she said with a smile he couldn't see. The young teen then picked up her pace and jogged off into the summer darkness.

CHAPTER FIVE

Miss Lakely looked especially attractive on the next to last day of school. Her silky, honey-blonde hair and green eyes sparkled as she greeted the homeroom class in the morning. She wore a mint-colored, cotton blouse topping a pair of summer-white, linen slacks. Her white, open-toed sandals complimented her outfit.

The students ambled into the classroom for the brief homeroom session before the first block classes of the day. Becky and her friend, Jen, were chatting when the class wise-ass, Eddie McKinnon, approached the two girls.

The disheveled boy with the devilish smile and reputation shared the same homeroom. He quickly sidestepped in front of Becky, blocking her path as she stepped toward her desk.

"Hey, Bing, I got a question for you," he said. "And I've been thinking about it for a long time."

The two girls immediately became stone-faced, anticipating some offensive remark to come out from the obnoxious classmate.

"Oh? What has your tiny, twisted mind been thinking about for a long time?" Becky replied.

"I just wondered if you and your family eat everything with chopsticks. I mean, how the hell do Chinese people like you eat something like pudding or oatmeal using chopsticks? I'm guessing you have to use forks and spoons sometimes."

"Oh, Eddie, you're such a freakin' tool! Just crawl back into your hole," Jen said.

"But wait a minute, Jen. Our friend, Eddie here has just asked me a very good question."

She then turned to face the provoking young man. "You see, Eddie, we Chinese don't eat *everything* with chopsticks. Sometimes when we eat, we simply pick up our food with our hands just like you do!" Becky told him, not hiding her triumphant smirk and giggle.

Jen laughed out loud.

"All right, gang, let's all take our seats. The beginning bell will ring soon," Miss Lakely announced.

After recording the daily attendance, she asked for silence so the morning notices could be heard over the public address system's speaker.

The fifty-five-year-old administrator, Principal Alfonse "Al" Pratt, congratulated the senior class with his familiar, baritone voice. The wall speakers again echoed through the building while he expressed how he and the faculty looked forward to the commencement ceremony later that evening at six o'clock. He further wished the rest of the student body a pleasant and safe summer, announcing he'd see them again in September to begin the next school year.

He made no additional reference to the tragic loss of graduating senior, Cindy Shea.

Before the tone sounded to begin the day's shortened classes, Amanda Lakely asked for attention from her homeroom class.

"Are there any students being dismissed early today? I just need to know who won't be returning to the homeroom at the end of the day."

"Ah, Miss Lakely, I have….ah, actually Becky and I both have band practice for tonight's graduation ceremony. We won't be back for homeroom period this afternoon," Andy announced.

"Oh, yes, thank you, Andrew," the stylish teacher replied, jotting a few notes in her attendance book.

* * *

Later that afternoon, the North Haven High School football field was neatly trimmed and modestly decorated with flowers surrounding the national, state of Connecticut, and town flags that hung from the tall, white pole. The playing field's thick grass had never looked greener in preparation for the ceremony. The event involved local dignitaries, the audience, some alumni, and the graduates. A temporary platform faced hundreds of folding chairs evenly spaced over the natural verdant carpet.

The early evening was comfortable since last night's storm had ushered in a pleasant, cool front. Gratefully, the outdoor graduation ceremony was brief and started promptly at five PM. The class valedictorian, town mayor, and Principal Pratt appeased the audience with their brief speeches.

Most of the North Haven High School faculty members attended the ceremony. Their cordial smiles spoke of their happiness for the senior class graduates, their families, and the beginning of a much needed summer vacation. During her speech, the valedictorian asked for a brief moment of silence to remember the one senior, Cindy Shea, who wouldn't walk with her classmates tonight. The tragedy was still raw and in the minds of students and adults alike.

Becky sat several rows in front of Andy with the other flautists in the high school band. In between musical performances they texted each other, as did most of the students, communicating with friends on the field and in the stands.

Becky texted: **my dad came to watch the grads and our band. He's driving me home. Let's meet in parking lot near rear gate?**

Andy responded: **sounds good! my mom drove me. we can make plans for 2nite in the lot!**

After the ceremonial closing and the band playing the traditional "Pomp and Circumstance" piece ended, the crowd, the graduates, and band members all mingled on the football field, eventually filing out of the stadium. Kisses, hugs, and handshakes defined the energy.

As Andy strolled off of the field with his encased coronet, his cell rang. "Meet me by the War Memorial!" Becky said quickly, then disconnected.

A small, park-like meditation area was the focal point at the far end of the gravel parking lot. It had a landscaped garden with lush, green grass and a few wrought-iron benches for people to sit, to rest, and to meditate. Vibrant summer flowers encircled the granite monument. The polished stone was engraved with names of the North Haven men and women who had lost their lives in military conflicts.

Becky soon approached Andy, already sitting on a bench. As usual, he appeared to be in deep thought. His coronet case and band uniform plumed-hat rested beside him. She set down her flute case before sitting next to him. Without a word, they both stared out at the parking lot with the crowd of families getting into their cars before exiting.

"Hey, Andy, just think! We'll be wearing those graduation caps and gowns two years from now."

Andy's face briefly grinned but then morphed back into a more serious expression.

"Look, Beck, I've been thinking about this. You really don't have to go back to Hook Island tonight with me, if…if you don't want to go." He then nervously fumbled with his coronet case.

She sensed her friend was simply being polite, trying to act like an independent, courageous young gentleman. He was offering a slim window of opportunity to back out of her commitment she had made last night on the squishy walk home.

Deciding to tease his feelings a bit, she responded with a question.

"But if I don't go with you, will you go out there all by yourself into that creepy, dirty, old factory to look for your camera?"

She watched as Andy swallowed hard with his Adam's apple falling and rising.

Hearing her accurate words sent a nervous shiver down his spine. He turned to face his petite friend.

"Ah, um...sure. I can just go out there tonight, retrieve my camera from inside the factory and then get the hell out of there. I'm sure I'll be back at my home before nine."

Becky tested him once again.

"Are you sure you want to go out to Hook all alone, Andy?"

"Who, me? Oh, sure!" he responded nervously, avoiding her eyes. "But you know if *you did want* to come with me, you can. I mean, if you got nothing else going on tonight. It's just a quick trip over the bridge, you know. At least tonight there'll be no cops and no freakin' rain! So, it's up to you, Beck, if you want to join me or not."

The corners of Becky's mouth curled up as she looked across at the taller Andrew Abbot and his attempted bravado. She sensed his anxiety about returning to the creepy island factory alone. It was obvious he had just proposed a subtle plea for her to join him. Without a Bumper Stone or Becky Bing by his side, he'd have to somehow get inside the decrepit, dark building and crawl around the crumbling, old factory by himself. She knew her friend quite well and how ill-equipped he was for such an adventure. Andy had a lot of good traits, but bravery wasn't one of them.

For a moment she remained silent, not wanting to answer him too quickly. She stood up and then reached for her flute case. She looked at his expression of anticipation, waiting anxiously for her response. But she wanted to continue the tease just a bit longer. She began pacing back in forth in her well-pressed band uniform, feigning a quiet moment to herself to think. Then she made a theatrical, audible sigh before answering.

"Yeah, well, maybe I'll go out there with you tonight. Besides, I already told you last night that I'd join you. And don't forget, I have to get my bicycle back sooner or later."

Andy didn't try to hide his relieved expression. His face lit up with a beaming smile. They began strolling toward the few remaining parked cars. Families and friends were leaving the lot in their vehicles for dinners, parties, and other festivities to celebrate a loved one's milestone.

"We'll meet at the corner of Bridge Street, eight o'clock sharp," she said, with the tone of a military drill sergeant.

"Okay!" the relieved young man replied.

Becky soon spotted her father, Dr. Wei Jiang Bing, leaning against his shiny, champagne-colored Lincoln Continental. She waved to him, catching his attention.

The two teens slowly walked away from the memorial garden. Then something startled them to stop in their steps.

The roaring sound of a motorcycle engine starting up made them turn their heads to look behind them. They spotted a man dressed in a black, short-sleeved, silk shirt, with blue jeans topping off black leather boots. A puff of thin, white smoke escaped the muffler of the Yamaha FZ-1 he straddled. His back was toward them so they couldn't see his face. But they noticed his forearms were covered in colorful tattoos. As they slowly walked by him, gently swinging their encased instruments, they both turned to look into the face that went with the body.

The rugged face and the shoulder-length, black hair was unmistakable. The tattooed biker was the same man seen last evening as he walked off of Hook Island.

The rider soon noticed their stares. He smiled politely and nodded toward them. It was obvious he didn't recognize them as the two bicyclists from the previous night on the island. It would be difficult since they were now wearing their school band uniforms.

Not a word was said as Becky then jogged across the nearly emptied parking lot to meet her father.

Andy stepped slowly across the gravel ground toward his mother's car.

His mom was chatting with another parent through opened car windows. He politely waved then pulled open the rear door, placed his coronet case inside, then slipped into the front passenger seat. While fastening his seat belt, he shot a deliberate glance to where the long-haired, tattooed man sat on his shiny, motorcycle.

But the mysterious stranger was no longer there. The muscular biker was already gone from the North Haven football stadium lot.

CHAPTER SIX

There was still ample June daylight at eight o'clock when Becky and Andy once again crossed the wooden bridge leading to Hook Island. This time they traveled on foot and walked briskly to burn off nervous energy.

"Hey, Beck, why the hell do you think that same guy we saw walking around here last night was sitting on the Harley at the graduation ceremony tonight? You know, that dude with the tats all over his arms."

She barely managed to keep pace beside her long-striding friend as they walked along.

"Well, first of all, it wasn't a Harley. It was a Yamaha bike. And, he could have been there for many reasons. Maybe he had a kid or niece or a nephew graduating."

"Yeah, but geez, did you notice the huge biceps on that guy? They stretched out the sleeves on his shirt, for God's sake! I wouldn't want to mess with that freakin' dude. And I'm glad he wasn't involved with that bust last night."

Becky smiled, stealing a glance over at Andy's thin, wiry arms and practically non-existent bicep muscles.

After they walked across the bridge toward the abandoned factories, they picked up their pace. As they did so, they kept a vigilant watch for anyone who might be on the island.

"I think the more important question is—what *did* happen here last night? There wasn't anything in this morning's *Register* about the police raid out here," Becky said, picking up their conversation.

"I guess they just got warned or probably the cops cited the band and groupies for trespassing onto the old factory property. You know, like we trespassed."

Becky's eyes rolled over toward her friend.

"Yeah, but they might have also got them on dope charges, too. Some of those groupies were smokin' pot! I'm just glad nobody caught us hiding outside. And that makes me think of something else. Any more word from our buddy who got us involved with this caper, Mr. Bumper Stone?"

"Oh, yeah. I got another text from him earlier today. There's no change in his grandfather's condition but he told me he's not expected to pull through. His grandpa is his mom's father. She, of course, wants to be by his side, as does Bumper. Although the trip is serious, he also told me that he's having a lot of fun running around with new friends down in New York City."

"Oh…that's too bad about his grandfather. And it really isn't such a great way to begin summer vacation."

Approaching building C1, they walked up to the same alleyway where they had hid their bicycles the evening before. They both breathed a quiet sigh of relief when they spotted the bikes still standing where they had left them. And, as they turned to the left, they saw the factory window was still left opened.

When they cautiously walked around to the opposite side of the building, they discovered the factory's main entranceway. But their eyes zoomed only onto a shiny, new padlock securing the door handles. There was also a new, official North Haven Police sign stapled to the door. In large, red letters it read "Trespassers will be prosecuted."

"That lock looks pretty new to me," Andy said.

"Yeah, I bet the cops had someone install it earlier today, after last night's raid."

The young duo carefully skirted the entire building, finding the same setup at the rear entrance to the building—another shiny new lock and a "No Trespassing" sign. They eventually walked completely around the weathered structure until they returned to the opened window once again. Peeking inside, they could see nothing but complete darkness. With no interior lights on, it was difficult to make out anything inside the lower level factory floor. The only natural light came from the little sunlight fading through the opened window.

"Becky, I'm gonna have to squeeze through this window and try to climb down to the factory floor. Even though we can't see it now, I remember exactly where my camcorder landed. It's on that huge pile of cloth material just below us."

"Geez, Andy, are you sure about getting down to the factory floor? I mean, there's nothing to grip onto while you shimmy down. It's got to be at least a fifteen foot drop down to that old pile of material."

"Yeah, I know, but let me try. And besides, I have no choice. I've got to get my new camera back. My parents gave it to me for my sixteenth birthday."

Andy easily twisted and slithered his long, lean body through the rusty window frame. He maneuvered himself inside the factory then dropped his legs straight down below him. As his hands tightly gripped the window sill, his knuckles turned a bloodless white.

"Ah, this is great! My foot just felt an old, metal heating pipe. I can stand on it then crouch down to hang by my hands from it. Then I can just drop down."

"Are you sure?" Becky watched her friend as he contorted into a human pretzel below her. He slowly brought one hand down to his feet, balancing precariously on the old steam heating pipe.

In the still darkness, only the muffled sounds of Andy's grunts and groans could be heard. But those expressions soon climaxed with a much louder...

"Oh, no.... ooooohh shit!"

"What? What the hell's the matter?" Becky asked nervously.

But there was no immediate answer.

The next sound was the creaking and crumbling of rusted old pipe. She knew it was bending under Andy's weight. Suddenly it collapsed, breaking off into sections. She instinctively reached down to grab her friend's hand. But it was too late.

His body fell quickly. But there was no other sound from Andy after he hit bottom.

Becky stuck her head through the open window, but still could not make out anything in the darkness below.

Fortunately, Andy made a soft landing on the stacked pile of old textile material, the same cloth remnants that caught his camcorder for a safe landing just twenty-four hours earlier.

"Andy, Andy, are you all right?" Becky shouted down into the pitch black factory.

"Huh? Damn! Yeah, I'm okay. I just twisted my ankle in the fall, but it's...it's all right."

"Can you find your camcorder?"

The scratching sound of Andy crawling on the pile of canvas-like cloth was the only sound Becky could hear from down below.

"Yeah, I just found it!"

"Listen, Andy, with that pipe broken, there's no freakin' way for you to climb back up here. And we already know the doors are all padlocked."

"No kidding! But, maybe I can bust open one of those old doors."

A silent pause followed.

"No, no! Geez, don't do that! The cops could get us on destructive vandalism on top of trespassing. We could be in a ton of trouble. Listen, I just got an idea. Do you remember when we just walked around the building? In the parking lot, there was some sort of metal hatchway leading down to the lower level of the factory. I noticed it had a recessed handle to it. I might be able to lift it open and climb down to meet you there."

"Yeah, Becky, I saw that hatchway plate in the ground, too. It was kinda big. Maybe it was used for deliveries or something."

"Now, do you think you can walk over in that direction to where it is?"

"How the hell can I do that? I can't see a blasted thing. It's pitch black down here! And I sure as hell don't know where there are any light switches!"

"And you don't want to turn any lights on even if you could find the switch. But you can use the light from your cell phone. You should be able to get enough light from your screen. And your BlackBerry is just like mine. It has a compass 'app' in the tools option to direct you to the hatchway."

"Okay, but what the hell direction do I follow to get to the hatchway? I can't see my hand in front of me down here."

"Ah...damn, let me think for a minute. We know the sun comes up over Hook Island each morning, so that's the east. Assuming it is due east, the metal plate would be a little to the south. So, use your compass to walk in a kinda, you know, southeasterly direction."

She looked down below into the factory and saw a small, bright light emanate from Andy's cell device.

"Okay, I got the compass working and now I'm walking, ah...I'm going in the ah...ah...southeast direction. Becky, when you get to the metal plate, bang on it with a rock or something. That'll help me pinpoint where it is."

"Will do!" She said and quickly left the opened window, scooting around the building to the metal hatchway. It was easy to find in the fading light, as the sun had not set completely.

Andy took tentative steps with one foot in front of the other using the limited light from his BlackBerry. He eased across the factory floor, often stumbling over deep divots in the crumbled cement deck. At one time he bumped into a wooden support that went from floor to ceiling. He later crashed head-on into a steel piece of antiquated textile machinery, still smelling of motor grease and oil. This was soon followed with him accidentally kicking an empty beer bottle, presumably discarded from the previous night's jamming session.

As he moved along through the eerie darkness with only a tiny source of dim light, a sudden noise startled him as it echoed in the canyon of the abandoned factory. He immediately froze in place realizing he was not alone.

The noise repeated again and again in rapid succession. He determined the sound was coming from Becky banging on the metal hatchway plate. With a sigh of relief, he called her from his cell phone.

"Beck, I can hear your banging noise and think I know where it's coming from. I should be over there soon."

"Good! Hey, I just got the underground shaft doors lifted. And there's a steel ladder attached to the wall leading down inside. I'm climbing down and will meet up with you."

"Okay, but…but…please be careful, Becky."

They disconnected.

But Andy paused after he spoke the words of caution to his friend. It struck him how intensely he had meant what he said to her.

Becky also heard the sensitive concern in his voice, then closed her cell and cautiously stepped down the rusted old ladder.

Andy continued limping across the black nothingness using minimal weight on his now swelling ankle. Then he heard Becky's voice echo in the darkness.

"Andy, Andy! Are…are you here?"

"Yeah, yeah, I'm over here, but I can't see you. Put your cell on for some light."

Andy kept moving gingerly and then saw a quick flash of light, then darkness.

"Hey, Becky, keep it on. I just saw it flash for a second then it went out. What the hell did you do, turn it on then shut it off?"

"Huh? What are you talking about? I haven't even taken it out of my pocket yet. You must be seeing things!"

Andy limped closer to her voice, knowing he wasn't just seeing things. He was certain there had been a sudden flash of light coming from somewhere.

Finally, the two illuminated cell phones were in sight, dancing around in the factory darkness with every hand movement. Becky stepped closer toward Andy's light. Her hand reached out to touch him. When she felt his bare arm, she grasped it tightly.

"How's your sprained ankle? We gotta get you home soon to ice it up!"

"Yeah, just lead me over to the ladder and let's get the hell out of here!"

Suddenly they heard a loud, flapping noise, followed by a breezing whoosh going past them, stopping them in their tracks. With the infinite darkness, they couldn't make out what had just soared by their heads. The shock of the noise and breeze froze the two of them in place.

"What...what the hell was that?" Andy asked, nervousness ringing in his voice.

"I...I think it was a freakin' bat!"

"Oh...shit, no, I hate bats. Where's that ladder? We gotta get to the ladder."

"Here, hold my hand and I'll lead us back to it."

Andy felt the warmth of Becky's hand holding his while they cautiously walked toward the hidden escape shaft. Despite the nerve-racking situation, and his painful ankle, her soft, smooth hand felt good—now tightly intertwined with his own.

"Here, it's over here. I left the shaft's metal cover pried opened a bit. It's too dark outside now for any light to come through, but I thought we could at least smell the salty, fresh air outside to lead us back to the ladder."

Andy remained silent, quietly impressed with Becky's sharp mind. He knew she was gifted academically, as was he, but this type of intelligence didn't come from textbooks and homework.

Just before they were about to climb up the steel-rung ladder to the hatchway, a light once again flickered in what appeared to be an underground tunnel.

"What the hell is that?" Andy whispered to Becky. "There's a light somewhere down that alley. What is that anyway? Is it some sort of tunnel?"

"I don't know and I really don't give a damn," Becky replied. "Let's just climb up this ladder and get our butts out of here!"

"Wait, wait," Andy said, slipping his hand from Becky's. "It doesn't make sense. Why would there be some light coming from that dark tunnel? I think we should check it out. We won't be coming back here again. And, the curiosity will bother me for a long time," he joked.

"Yeah, just like the curious cat, my friend. And remember what happened to him!"

"C'mon," Andy persuaded, now grabbing Becky's hand tighter and pulling it toward him.

The two stepped cautiously through the dark, underground, limestone tunnel. But now their cell phone lights were turned off. They didn't need it. They moved quietly toward a dim beam of light. It seemed to come from a source at a right angle to the narrow tunnel.

The only noise they could hear now was their own nervous breathing in the dank, musty-smelling tunnel. As they came closer to the light, they realized the tunnel did turn at a sharp corner. When they reached the junction Andy leaned against the wall and then slowly stretched his neck around the corner of the tunnel.

Within seconds, he brought his head back around, still keeping his back flat against the wall.

"What is it, Andy? Can you see where the light's coming from?"

"Ah…yeah. There's…there's some kind of room at the end of this next tunnel. The room's door has an old, dirty, glass window. The light's coming from inside that room and through the window," he responded in a low, soft voice.

"Okay, now we know where it comes from. Let's split and get back home!"

"What do you think that room is? Is there anyone inside there?" Andy whispered.

"I have no idea, but c'mon, let's find out!"

Andy crouched down and waddled like a duck along the adjacent, shorter tunnel. Becky did the same, following right behind him.

The door to the lit room was only ten yards away. When they finally reached it, they remained in a crouching position below the single-paned glass window. They weren't quite ready to stand up and peek inside.

Then they heard the voice. Although the voice was muffled through the door, it sounded familiar to the two young sleuths. As they heard more of the speaker through the door, they turned to look at one another, grabbing each other's arms.

The person on the other side of that door was someone they both knew quite well.

CHAPTER SEVEN

Upon hearing the familiar voice, each of the two teenagers slowly straightened up from their low hunkering position. They now stood with their faces nearly pressed to the glass door window trying to make out what was going on inside the room.

There were layers of grease, grime and dust layered and smudged on the old, glass window. The condition made it difficult to see anything inside clearly.

First, Becky peeked carefully. She knew the darkness behind them and the light in the room would prevent anyone inside from seeing their silhouettes.

They peered in, looking at what appeared to be an old, abandoned, administrative office. There were a few older, battleship-grey metal desks and tables with small, green-shaded desk lamps. High tiers of metal file cabinets lined most of the far wall.

Squinting through the clouded, dirty glass, the image of the individual was blurry, but the mint-green top, white linen slacks, and voice belonged unmistakably to their beloved homeroom teacher, Miss Amanda Lakely.

The honey-blonde-haired woman was talking on a cell phone while perched over a laptop. She sat at an old grey, metal office desk. But what seemed odd was the cell phone wasn't her candy-apple, red iPhone. The cell model she held was a cheap, plain model with a dull, blue casing.

The two could eavesdrop on the phone conversation although the voice was still muffled, echoing inside the lifeless office. They could make out the image of their homeroom teacher as she spoke.

"Yeah, I'm all set here for tonight. Yeah, it went well. Okay, but we have to meet on this real soon. Things are getting too hot around here and I don't want any fuck-ups at this point. We've worked too hard to get where we are today. We need to discuss everything in detail before the deal is made."

There was a brief pause.

"Sure. Let's meet here on Monday afternoon, say at three o'clock...good! See you then."

The teacher flipped the cell phone closed and quickly stood up. Becky and Andy suddenly panicked, anticipating Miss Lakely would now come out through the same office door they were leaning against. They quickly dropped down, and quickly duck walked back through the dark and musty tunnel. After making the turn down the main tunnel, they flipped open their BlackBerry devices to light the way.

When they finally reached the steel ladder attached to the cement wall, Andy stopped with his foot on the first rung.

"Hey, do you hear anything?" Andy whispered.

"No, I don't hear anything," she responded softly.

"Yeah, that's right. Miss Lakely isn't coming out this way. She's not following us. So, she didn't come out through that dirty, old office door we were leaning against."

"Shh! Wait, listen!" Becky said.

The sound of a car starting its engine roared. They froze in place not knowing where the vehicle was parked. Then the sound of tires squealing told them their homeroom teacher was already on her way driving off Hook Island.

Without speaking a word, the two climbed up and out through the hatchway. Together they slid back the metal hatch cover into its place. Then they stepped into the twilight, and headed for the alley to retrieve their hidden bicycles.

They didn't speak while they pedaled over the wooden bridge and finally off of the island. They put on the brakes when they reached the corner at Bridge Road in the Beechwood Knoll section of town. Before splitting off to their respective homes, Andy turned to face Becky while adjusting his helmet under the streetlight.

"Well, at least I picked up my camcorder."

Becky's eyebrows arched at the remark.

"Andy, we picked up a lot more than your freakin' camcorder! I'm still blown away seeing Miss Lakely in that...that hidden underground office! I mean, what the hell do you think she was doing down there?"

She could see Andy's blank look under the corner streetlamp.

"I don't have a clue, Beck. And we sure as hell can't come right out and ask her because we weren't supposed to be there either. In a way, we were spying on her. Geez, it's gonna be weird seeing her again in our first summer Logic class next Monday morning."

Becky paused before commenting.

"And, it'll be weirder seeing her again—at that factory office on Monday afternoon at three o'clock," she said, with a grin. With that, she turned and pedaled away from her friend to get home to her parents.

* * *

Once again, Miss Lakely was smiling as she sat at her classroom desk in Room 205. She greeted the students as they came in for the first session of the Advanced Program's "Introduction to Logic" course.

Besides Becky Bing and Andrew Abbot, there were three other students.

The strikingly handsome Tyler Farnham sat directly in front of the teacher's desk. He was now entering the twelfth grade and certain to be elected President of the

Senior Class. Amber Woods, the most attractive girl in the senior class, and possibly the entire school, took a seat at the rear of the classroom. Hans Schmidt, a junior, was the fifth student. He was barely five feet tall, with a close crop of blonde hair; he wore thick eyeglasses, and had a perennial smile on his youthful face.

"I want to welcome you all to your first class of Intro to Logic," Miss Lakely began. "I assure you, it won't be like anything you've ever studied before. First of all, there is no textbook for this summer's four-week accelerated course. The only resources you'll need are access to the Internet along with good listening and note-taking skills.

"As you already know, you'll get one college credit upon passing this course. And being an advanced program, I want to conduct this class as if you are mature college students. I believe that you all deserve to be treated like the young adults you are.

"If on some comfortable days you'd like to meet outside, away from the school building, we can do that. If you want to bring into class a coffee or cold drink, you may do so. If you need to use the lavatory, just get up and leave. You'll also notice I wrote my personal email address on the board. In the event that you must miss class or if you have some personal issues, you can send me an email. I will get back to you as soon as possible."

Miss Lakely then stood up and walked around to the front of her desk. Each of the five students gawked in surprise at the young teacher's outfit as she strutted toward the neatly lined up rows of desks. With summer school starting, the dress regulations were relaxed for students and teachers alike. She was dressed in a pair of dark cranberry, very short-shorts, contrasting with her heather-colored, short-sleeved prairie top. The colors complimented her well-tanned arms and long, shapely legs. The shorts barely came down past her pelvic area.

The outfit clearly fit her body well and enhanced her youthful figure.

"Now, most of these class sessions will be a group discussion format. And the first principle I want you to know is with logic, you must *always, always* have an open mind. That means you never attempt to solve problems with prejudice or assumption."

The students were riveted onto the young teacher's discourse.

"All of you already understand prejudice. It comes from the word prejudge. And, if we prejudge, we can never solve problems. And, prejudice creates or results in more problems. And these problems may surface in social, economical, mathematical, and especially, logical spheres. Remember, prejudice prevents us from arriving at correct conclusions using sound logic.

"Now, another pitfall we must avoid is making assumptions. *Assuming* is a common error that many people commit when trying to logically solve problems. You can think of assumptions as the natural enemy to good, logical analysis. You can't assume something without proving and verifying it before answering a problem correctly in processing logic."

Miss Lakely now turned around to erase her email address from the board. She picked up a red marker pen and wrote on the classroom's whiteboard using oversized letters, 'ASS U ME.'

"You all must know the old expression and keep it in mind: when we assume, we...." The teacher paused.

"Make an ass of you and me," the class responded in a loud harmony, giggling.

"Now remember that one! It'll be the easiest question on your first pop quiz."

"Miss Lakely, can you tell us how this Logic course will help us in our future careers, you know, after we complete college and go out into the real world?" Tyler Farnham asked.

"Sure, Tyler. Good logic training can help anybody in just about every profession. It is integral to engineering, especially software engineering, law, medicine, architecture, construction, scientific research, and in every job that requires *diagnostic analysis*. And, I'm sure you've all seen those popular Crime Scene Investigation shows. So, good logic is essential in forensic medicine and every type of detective work when solving complex mysteries. But you're going to learn that good, sound reasoning and logic pertains to not just professional careers but everything in life!"

She then continued to lead an open discussion providing scenarios where logical reasoning would affect every aspect of life. The students enjoyed the interactive dialogue and the opportunity to vocally participate. The only student who remained quiet during the class was the beautiful, strawberry-blonde senior, Amber Woods.

At the end of class period, the students talked among themselves while exiting the school building. The consensus was they all had enjoyed the first class, the group discussions, and of course, their teacher, the energetic Miss Lakely.

Becky followed Andy as they threaded their way once again by Peck's Pond. As they passed the body of water she asked, "So, are you going back to Hook Island later today?"

"Huh? Oh, I don't know. I was thinking about it. It really is none of our business what goes on out there. Maybe Miss Lakely has a part time job working there for the summer. You know that teachers aren't highly paid. She might be just picking up some extra cash."

"Job? Extra cash? Are you kidding me? What...on Hook Island? C'mon, Andy! Jump up onto the 'Clue Bus' for God's sake! Did you see any signs of a business operating down in that dirty, crumby basement? Were there any other people around? There's no legitimate business going on down there. Miss Lakely is up to something that's freakin' mysterious! And judging from her language on the phone, she wasn't taking a customer service call.

Nobody, and I mean nobody, should be down there. There is no way a legal business would be down in that...that bat-infested factory. Those dilapidated buildings are *condemned* for God's sake!"

"What are you saying, Beck? What do mean—no legal business? Do you think Miss Lakely is into some criminal shit or something?"

Becky just shrugged her shoulders.

"Hell, I don't know. But it's kinda weird we came across our favorite teacher inside that old, dingy, underground office. And I'm sure only you and I know about her after-school activities, whatever they are. I know it's her personal business what she does outside of North Haven High, but if she's into something that's breaking the law, we kinda have a civic responsibility to report it."

Andy brushed away some tall weeds as he continued forward along the path.

"Hmm. You could be right about that. But I hope you're wrong. I suppose if we did get there before she returned at three o'clock we could eavesdrop in that dark tunnel way again."

They changed topics for the remainder of the walk home. At this point everything was merely speculation. They chatted about the other members of their Logic class. It was obvious they all had enjoyed the class and looked forward to the next session the following morning. Finally they reached the point where they split up on their walk home.

"Okay, so we can make one more trip out to Hook Island. I'll meet you at the corner of Bridge Rd. Say about two-fifteen?" Becky asked.

"Cool. See ya' then."

Their heads weren't as light on this afternoon as they walked in different directions toward their homes. Each was burdened with the thoughts of their favorite teacher involved with some criminal activity. There was no mistake they'd seen and heard a different woman when Miss Lakely was on the blue cell phone in that underground office. It was her voice, but eerily didn't seem to be her warm and witty persona they observed each day in the classroom.

That afternoon, the two teens followed their same routine, hiding their bikes in the narrow alley between the abandoned buildings. After panning around for any sign of other life, they ran quickly over to the in-ground hatchway. Carefully, they opened the metal-covered hatchway and climbed down the rusted, steel ladder. Andy managed to pull the hatch cover back in place.

Today, Andy had remembered to bring a small but intensely bright flashlight from home. The light beam pierced the creepy darkness, scattering spiders, centipedes, and other insects clinging to the dank, limestone walls. They quickly found the hidden tunnel and moved to position themselves near the old office before their teacher would return at three o'clock.

Andy stopped in his tracks, forcing Becky to bump into his backside.

"Hey, Beck," he said in a soft tone. "I just figured out what the heck these tunnels are! They're old steam heating tunnels. Look up on the wall." He flashed the light above the two of them, scattering some crawling insects. "Those are old-fashioned insulated steam pipes. They were used to carry heat to all of these factory buildings. Look, there are water pipes and old electrical cables running through here as well."

"Yeah, that makes sense, Andy," Becky whispered in return. "Older building complexes and factories like this had steam tunnels to heat different buildings from a single power plant. That way each building didn't have to have its own furnace or boiler. My dad told me how the Yale University campus in New Haven has the same setup. A big, central furnace heated all of the dormitories and buildings through a network of underground steam tunnels."

"Yeah, well, this particular steam tunnel leads to our mysterious teacher, Amanda Lakely."

The grimy office door was still closed. Nothing could be seen inside since no lights were on inside.

"Hey, if she didn't come in through the hatchway like we did and the two main entrances are locked, how the hell do you think she gets in and out of this office?"

"I don't have a clue how those other buildings are connected. We only explored Building C1 because of the secret mission our good buddy, Bumper, sent us on."

"Yeah, that son-of-a....."

The creaking sound of a door opening interrupted the comment. A soft click of a wall switch followed with overhead lights coming on inside the office.

They both peered in through the nearly opaque, clouded window to once again see their teacher. She had changed her outfit and was now wearing blue jeans and a black, short-sleeved jersey with a designer logo on the back neckline. Stepping directly to the same metal desk, she placed a black canvas bag on the surface. They watched quietly as she unzipped the bag, extracting her laptop computer.

Becky looked down and checked her cell's display. It was exactly one minute past three in the afternoon.

While Miss Lakely began tapping on the computer keyboard, the door on the far wall once again opened and shut quickly. Although the grimy window blurred much of the image, the physical characteristics of the man could be identified. He had shoulder length, black hair. His short-sleeve polo shirt displayed forearms covered with multi-colored tattoos.

"Look! It's...it's that same biker dude!" Andy whispered to Becky.

"Shh!"

They each pressed their ears against the base of the thick wooden door.

"Thanks for getting here on time, Jack," Miss Lakely said without looking up.

The biker dude now has a name, Jack.

"Amanda, listen. I just wanted to talk to you about what's goin' on here. Things are getting too damn hot right now and I don't like it. I want to move quickly before we blow the whole thing."

"Look, Jack, I know you're uptight right now. But we have to remain cool and stick to the plan. We have too much invested. It's gone so well up 'til now and we don't want to screw it up."

"Yeah, but I just want to finish this job and get the hell out of this town. That accident the other night still bothers the shit out of me. That could have been prevented," Jack said with conviction in his voice.

"Listen, we don't know exactly what went down that night. But until we know more, you've got to chill out for God's sake, or you'll blow every fucking thing we've worked on for months."

"I don't agree, Amanda," Jack replied, raising his voice a few octaves. "I'm getting too nervous about this shit. This place is too hot now, especially with that rock band bringing the local cops here and raiding the other building! That was too close for comfort."

"I know, I know. But don't go doing anything stupid, Jack. We can't screw up all that we've planned. And, we still have more work to do before we do what we came here for."

"I...I think you're wrong. I think we can pull this off now. I want to get the hell out of here and get back home to Chicago as soon as possible."

"Jack, don't go stupid on me! We've got to be patient, for God's sake. We have a plan, a good plan, and we have to stick to it!"

A pause hung in the air.

"Okay, Amanda, but I'm not going to be patient forever!" Jack responded with a defiant tone. "I've gotta get going. I have to meet the boss again tonight at his place. You know how he gets pissed if I'm late. "

The blurry image of Jack, the long-haired biker dude, could be seen storming out of the far office door. The door slammed loudly behind him.

Miss Lakely remained at the old, metal desk. She tapped something on her keyboard then closed her laptop and slid it into its black canvas carrying case.

Becky and Andy hadn't moved a muscle while they spied on the intriguing vignette unfolding inside the office. They now stared while their teacher raised a cell phone to her ear. But this time it wasn't the same blue-colored cell she used the first time they spotted her in the office. This time she held the candy-apple red iPhone she used in her classroom.

The two teens listened as she spoke in a subdued voice.

"Look, things are getting out of hand here real fast! Jack's acting a little too weird for me. In fact, he's rolling around like a freakin' loose cannon. I'm afraid he might do something stupid and blow the whole thing."

A muffled voice spoke to her over the cell.

"Okay, I'll take care of it as soon as I can. I'll get back to you!" Miss Lakely replied.

She snapped her red phone shut as she stood up, picked up her laptop case, and headed toward the far door. She turned off the light switch and was soon out of the office, slamming the door behind her.

Quietly, Becky and Andy retraced their steps with the flashlight leading them back to the hatchway ladder. Minutes later they heard their teacher's car peel out of the factory lot. Still without speaking, they eventually stepped up and out into the fresh air and slid the metal hatchway cover back in place. When they felt sure there wasn't anybody in sight, they ran back into the narrow alley to retrieve their hidden bicycles. Soon they were once again pedaling over the creaky, wooden bridge headed toward Beechwood Knoll.

"So, what the hell do you think that was all about?" Andy said peering over to his friend.

"Huh? Oh, God. I don't know," she replied, while pulling down her bike helmet's visor to block the afternoon sunlight.

"That sure as hell wasn't a pleasant conversation between Miss Lakely and Jack. And the other call wasn't much better."

"Yeah, and now I'm sure Jack wasn't hanging out at the graduation ceremony for some niece or nephew. When we saw him in the parking lot he was probably waiting up for Miss Lakely."

They cruised side by side along Bridge Street knowing they had uncovered something in which they shouldn't be involved. But that teasing mystery created a new thrill for each of them.

"Well, whatever the hell is going on, Andy, I think that it's none of our business. Remember, we just sorta got sucked into this...this situation. It began with Bumper and his sneaky videoing idea. If you hadn't dropped your camcorder we never would have returned to Hook Island. And now, we end up eavesdropping on our teacher doing something very private—you know kinda personal."

"Geez, Becky, you were the one who wanted to go back there today! Remember what you said about finding out what Miss Lakely was up to? You told me that if we discovered that she was doing something criminal, we should report it as part *of our civic responsibility*. Now, all of a sudden, you're changing your mind one-hundred and eighty degrees!"

"Yeah, yeah, I know, but now as far as I'm concerned, this story is over. We got the video for Bumper, we recovered your camera, and we got our bikes back! So, we finished what we intended to do on our trips out to the island. Unfortunately, while doing so, we learned that...that Miss Lakely has another life outside of Room 205. Now I feel we really have no business getting involved with what our teacher does on her own time. Besides, we didn't see her doing anything criminal. In fact, if you think about it, *we* are the only criminals here. *We* broke the law when *we* trespassed onto private property and broke into that old factory building. If you think about it, we committed the crime of 'breaking and entering.' Up until now, I had never done anything as stupid as this."

Andy chuckled as they slowed their bikes to a halt at an intersection stop sign. He turned to her to make a point.

"You know, Beck, you crack me up! You're always so...so practical and so..."

"Oh, ah ...so 'fuckin' law abiding'—to quote Bumper?" Becky interrupted.

Andy was startled at her edgy reply.

"Ah...no, no, Becky. I didn't mean it like that. I meant that you're practical in a good way. I happen to think you're right. We have no reason to spy or meddle into what Miss Lakely does. And, if I were a teacher, I wouldn't want any of my students snooping into my personal affairs outside of school." Becky smiled, knowing her friend spoke the truth. It was time to let it go. Let it go, at least for now.

"Hey, Andy, wanna come to my house for a cold drink before you head home for dinner?"

"Sure!"

The two parked their bikes to the side of the Bing driveway and entered through the breezeway door. Andy had never been inside Becky's house before. His eyes panned around each room as they made their way toward the kitchen.

When he entered the hardwood-floored kitchen, his eyes focused on an attractive, blonde-haired woman sitting at a granite-topped, center island counter. Her bright blue eyes matched the short-sleeved cotton blouse she wore over a khaki skirt. She was preparing a salad, slicing tomatoes and adding them to a large bowl of baby spinach. He initially thought the Bings might have a housekeeper and cook employed in their home.

Becky led Andy over to the woman. She then leaned into her and planted a kiss on her cheek.

"Hi, Mom! I'd like you to meet a good friend of mine. This is Andy Abbot."

The woman smiled warmly and then stood up to shake Andy's hand.

He knew his mouth was opened but he just couldn't seem to close it. He was totally surprised to see that Becky's mom was not Asian, but rather a strikingly attractive, Caucasian woman. He was taken with her sparkling blue eyes and how they complimented the blonde highlighted hair. His first thought was this woman could appear in movies with her looks.

"Pleased to meet you, Andy! I've heard so much about you and know you and Rebecca are classmates. And I understand you're in the marching band as well. Is it the trumpet you play?"

It took the young man a moment to engage his brain.

"Huh...oh, no...it's...it's the coronet. I play the coronet."

"Oh, how nice! But now I hear you're both in the same summer advance college credit program. Am I right that you're also taking the AP course in Logic?"

Andy gulped, agitating his Adam's apple, then stammered to get his answer out. His face was turning a light pink.

"Ah, yes, yes, ma'am, that's right."

Becky grinned, observing how socially awkward Andy was with her mother. She knew he never had problems socializing with adults in the past but now was having trouble answering simple questions. She compassionately intervened.

"Mom, we're going to get some lemonade then go up to my room to hang out for a while, okay?"

"Sure! And Andy, you're more than welcome to stay for dinner."

"Ah, ba, ah...no thanks, ah, Mrs. Bing. I'm expected home later on. Ba...but thanks anyway."

While Becky grabbed bottles of Snapple lemonade from the fridge, a loud news bulletin signal blared out from the small TV tucked into a corner of the kitchen counter.

The evening news anchorwoman from New Haven's Channel 8 interrupted the current program for the breaking announcement. Mrs. Bing and the teens stopped chatting to listen.

"There is an update on the tragic car accident that took place in North Haven earlier this week. We have just learned from the Medical Examiner's office that the body of the late North Haven High School teen, Cindy Shea, had a significant amount of illegal drugs in her system at the time of her death. The report came after an autopsy was performed. It appears that the vehicle Miss Shea was driving ran off at a curve. The Medical Examiner reported that the impact of the crash critically injured her brain and snapped her neck. The report also indicated the severed neck was the cause of death.

"According to police, the eighteen-year-old girl had attended North Haven School that day, but was never seen again after school dismissal. Nobody reported seeing Miss Shea drive her Toyota sedan away from the high school parking lot. The assumption is that the senior student had left school early and never returned home that day. The case is still under investigation. A private burial service for family members only, will be held later this week.

And now we return you back to our regular programming."

"Oh, that is so sad," Mrs. Bing commented with a sigh. "Did you know that young woman, ah...Cindy Shea, Andy?"

"Huh, ah no. No, I never met her."

"It's just so tragic," Mrs. Bing continued. "So, I guess there won't be a contingent of school classmates as the funeral service. The family wants it to be private. And that's certainly understandable."

Becky quietly led Andy up the carpeted staircase then down a long hallway. They each carried a bottle of lemonade.

She showed Andy into her bedroom and then closed the door for privacy.

The bedroom was large with several wall posters of Becky's heroes. There was a photo of a Taylor Swift concert taken somewhere in Rome, Italy; another of the Boston Pops performing at the legendary Tanglewood concert location in the Massachusetts Berkshires. There were oversized posters of other celebrities, too, including a large black and white print of an Albert Einstein photo.

Becky sat on her bed while Andy plopped in the chair near her computer desk. They both opened their Snapple drinks.

"Geez, Becky, I never figured that your mom, I mean...I just never...I never met your mother before," he finally blurted out.

Becky's smile turned into a laugh before she commented.

"You mean, you were surprised to see that my mother isn't Chinese like my dad and me!"

"Well...ya, I mean...it just didn't register when I first saw her that she...she was your mom."

Becky kept her smile while she spoke.

"I know, Andy. It completely showed on your face and the silly way you acted!" She chuckled once again. "And, do you know what you just did? You just fell into that trap of using poor logic."

"Huh?"

"See, you ASSUMED that my mother was going to be a short, Chinese woman with jet-black hair. You ASSUMED that's how my mother should look even before you met her. But your assumption was wrong and so you were taken off track. You were surprised at the facts. My mother isn't Chinese. She's an American Caucasian, has blonde, not black hair, and is almost five feet, nine inches tall.

"You know how we learned in class that *assuming* is a basic pitfall to avoid if we're going to become super detectives or analysts and use—good fundamental logic!"

"Okay, okay, I get it, I get it. And, and…I'm sorry," he replied with a sheepish grin.

Becky paused, creating a silence in her bedroom. She stared at her friend for a while before speaking again, but was now serious.

"You know, Andy, I never told this to anyone, but I never knew my real mother. For that matter, I never knew my biological father," she said in a soft voice.

Andy just looked at her, shocked at the personal revelation. He stared into her eyes before responding.

"Really?" Andy asked, a sensitive tone in his voice.

"Yeah, I was adopted by my American mother and Chinese American father. When they realized they couldn't conceive naturally they still wanted to have a child. So they decided to adopt. Together, they traveled to China to find a tiny, but ADORABLE, infant. And that abandoned, little baby girl was me!"

Becky put on a goofy, distorted expression and playfully crossed her eyes. Andy smiled at his friend's use of comedy with such a serious subject. He laughed at her expression then took a long slug of his lemonade.

"So you're adopted…and by some really neat parents. I think that's really, really cool!"

The teenagers hung out for nearly an hour in Becky's bedroom listening to music, talking about school, and other things they planned to do during their summer vacation. They purposely didn't bring up anything about Hook Island, Jack the biker, or Miss Lakely's mysterious role in the dingy, underground office. It was a time for two teenagers to chill out and talk about things that they liked, disliked, and hoped for, as their own futures unfolded. The time in Becky's bedroom provided the opportunity for them to get to know each other on a different level for the first time.

Later, Becky led her friend down the staircase.

Before leaving, he found Mrs. Bing sitting on the couch in the family room. Now more composed and confident, he thanked her for the hospitality.

"Oh, come anytime, Andy! And don't hesitate to join Becky here if you guys want to study together. I know how tough it can be to take a Logic course, especially during the hot days of summer!"

CHAPTER EIGHT

The next morning, Becky texted Andy while eating breakfast with her parents at the kitchen table. The text told him she had a dental cleaning in the morning and wouldn't be walking with him to summer school, but would meet him in class.

Since Andy walked alone with his long strides, the morning's trip didn't take long. He soon found himself to be the earliest student arriving on the school grounds. Sitting at a shaded picnic table at the side of the school building, he was startled when an unfamiliar voice yelled out from behind him.

"Mind if I join you before class starts, Andy?"

It was Tyler Farnham, the popular senior in his summer Logic class. He walked toward the picnic table and bench, setting down his capped Dunkin' Donuts coffee cup.

"Oh, ah sure, sure, have a seat, Tyler."

The two young men began chatting about the summer school course they shared inside Room 205.

"I especially like Miss Lakely teaching this class. She's young, interesting and is so totally hot," Tyler said.

"Yeah, I have her for my homeroom teacher," Andy responded. "And *she is* easy on the eyes. But I also like the Logic class she's teaching. We're lucky there are only five of us taking the course. And it seems we're all getting into the group discussion format or, as Miss Lakely calls it, the seminar format."

"Yeah, that's a cool way to teach a subject."

"I think everyone likes it, except maybe Amber Woods. Hey, you must know her, Tyler, you being a senior. I don't get it. Why...why is she so quiet in class? I mean, everyone gets into the discussion and chimes in, but Amber hardly ever says a freakin' word."

Tyler winced slightly at Andy's comment. Then he inhaled and sighed loudly before responding.

"I...I don't know for sure. But something weird is happening to Amber, or did happen to her."

"Did happen? What do you mean by that?"

"If you knew Amber as I have for several years, you'd realize she's one of the coolest kids at our school. And, she's obviously a good-looking chick, as you can see. But she's also smart; I mean really bright with a super personality. On top of all that, Amber is a good athlete. In fact, she was captain of the Ladies Golf team during her junior year."

"Hmm, I didn't know any of that."

"Amber could do anything she wanted to do. She's sure to get the 'Best Looking Girl" superlative title in our graduating class. I asked her in May if she was going to run for Class President, because if she did, she'd easily win. And of course I'd never consider running. But, she told me she wasn't interested and encouraged me to campaign for the office. So, I did."

Tyler paused, taking a swig from his Styrofoam coffee cup before continuing.

"Ya know, it's weird, Andy, her whole personality seemed to change back in April. Amber no longer talked with anyone after that. You could never find her after school. Even her closest friends were puzzled about the way she morphed into a hermit. It's almost as if during our spring vacation, someone *stole her soul.*"

Someone stole her soul.

Tyler's eerie but poetic words echoed in Andy's mind and sent an icy shiver down his spine. He now understood Amber's quiet behavior wasn't just superficial. There was something more serious that affected the attractive young girl with the emerald-green eyes and the curvy, hot figure.

"Tyler, you just said something happened to change Amber in the month of April, ah...during our school vacation. Do you know what the hell that was?"

As the two talked quietly, they were oblivious to other students arriving onto the school grounds. The teenagers hung around the school entrance, standing or sitting on the granite stone steps, waiting for the bell to allow them to walk through the main doors.

"I'm not sure what happened to Amber during that spring vacation period. I had traveled to London with my folks for that week. All I know is she stayed here and worked in the school's office to pick up some extra cash. I think she did some clerical work there. But to answer your question, I just really don't know what the hell happened to her that week."

A voice came from behind them.

"Hey! Are you guys ready to learn some logic?"

Becky Bing smiled at the two of them, waiting for them to join her on the walk into Miss Lakely's class.

Today, the stylish teacher wore beige cargo shorts with a black sleeveless top. The style provided a glimpse of the teacher's well-toned upper arms. Black earrings and black sandals matched her top.

"Now, today class, as part of some basic elements to our Introduction to Logic, I want to cover deductive and inductive reasoning. They're just two of the more common ways to employ good logic processing and to prove a hypothesis. Some of you may be familiar with these terms from your Geometry course. After we discuss them and the two methods are fully distinguishable, I want each of you to think of examples in your own lives where these logical pathways may have been used."

Although the five students were attentive and anxious to learn the methods of logic, they sensed something very different on this day in Room 205. And that difference had to do with Miss Lakely.

Her enthusiasm and trademark smile weren't present on this bright summer morning. Her washed out and tired appearance paralleled the lackluster energy when she spoke. On this morning she wore no makeup. There were deep, darkened circles around her eyes. It looked as though the young teacher hadn't slept much during the previous night.

The class period that day was boring and seemed to drag on. But the cloud of disinterest hanging in the room suddenly vanished with the jarring sound of emergency sirens.

The blaring noise from the police and fire vehicles echoed from across the street. The sound jerked the students out of their seats as. They joined Miss Lakely at the windows to see what caused the commotion. Each peered down the two stories focusing on several North Haven police cruisers and a Fire Rescue ambulance. They were all parked next to Peck's Park with all strobe lights working.

Miss Lakely stepped back from the windows and paused before her impromptu announcement.

"Okay, kids, let's....let's just call it a day! I'm dismissing you early this morning. I have a long drive to make now and had to leave a little early anyway. You all can investigate what's going on across the street and can report to me on the incident later."

"I bet a kid started another grass fire over there," offered the diminutive Hans Schmidt with his boyish grin.

The other students nodded in agreement since fires were often started in the park area. They usually ignited from a lit cigarette or were sometimes set purposely just to watch the fire engines disrupt classes at the high school.

"Okay, but please listen up before you all leave. For your homework, I want each of you to research on the Internet some definitions and examples of 'paradoxes.' We'll be going over these during our next class and how they play a role in Logic. After you understand what paradoxes are, give it some thought and keep this old expression in mind."

Miss Lakely then picked up a green dry-erase marker. She turned to write on the white board the following quote in oversized lettering:

THINGS AREN'T ALWAYS WHAT THEY SEEM TO BE

"This is something very important as you learn to use good logic. It will keep you in check so you don't run off to any premature conclusions in your problem-solving efforts."

She read the quote aloud to the students.

"Things aren't always what they seem to be."

The students jotted down the brief sentence before exiting the classroom to hustle across the street into Peck's Park.

Once outside the building, all five students jogged over toward the police cruisers to investigate the drama. Loud, unintelligible words squawked over the cars' two-way radio system. When Andy turned to look at the Fire Ambulance he noticed an underwater diver donning a wet suit and tugging on an oxygen tank over his shoulders.

"Look, Beck, there's a SCUBA diver. I wonder if somebody drowned in Peck's Pond. I bet he's going down to look for a body!"

"Yeah, but we can't get in too close with all of the crime scene tape hung up to keep away the crowd. Hey, I have an idea! Let's go around the corner and cut back through one of the openings in the bushes to get a better look."

"Cool!"

Without attracting attention, the two left their classmates and snuck around to the opposite side of the commotion. After finding a tight opening, they squeezed through the thick shrubbery and wild overgrown vegetation. Within minutes they were on the opposite side of Peck's Pond. They were hidden from the cops by the leafed-out trees and bushes. To lower their profile, they sat down on a thick, grassy slope that provided a good view of the pond and emergency activity. The two teens watched without saying a word.

The underwater diver immersed his body into the murky pond. The ripples disturbed the peaceful water, gently rocking the lily pads in the diver's wake. He swam closer toward the side of the pond where Becky and Andy were looking on.

He dove underwater for what seemed to be several minutes then suddenly popped up with a loud splash. His head swiveled then faced the other police and fire rescue personnel at the opposite shore. With a raised thumb of a gloved hand, he signaled that he had discovered something.

He dove under once again. He stayed underwater for a few minutes before emerging. But this time the resurfacing occurred more slowly.

And the diver wasn't alone.

Over his wetsuit-covered shoulders he carried up the drenched dead body of a man.

Becky and Andy quickly slid down the grassy slope on their butts for a better look.

The lifeless body slumped over the fireman's shoulders faced the diver's backside. The man's long, black hair was matted down with the swampy pond water. A dark colored t-shirt exposing both arms clung to him.

"Holy shit, Becky, take a look at those arms!"

The man's forearms, spattered with mud, had intricate tattoos in multi-colored designs. Although his body was limp they could still see that the man had a well-defined, muscular build. Then they saw something else as the diver repositioned the corpse over his shoulder. The victim was now directly facing the two teens on the slope.

In the middle of the man's pale forehead was a dark, bloodied hole.

"Oh my God, Andy! Look, look! It's…it's that guy, it's…it's Jack the biker!" Becky said, tugging forcefully on her friend's arm. "And he has a bullet hole in his head!"

The diver carried the dead body over his shoulder to the far shore to the awaiting police and rescue team.

Within minutes, the police cordoned off Peck's Pond with rolls of yellow crime scene tape. Meanwhile, a detective took nearly fifty photos of the corpse, the pond, and the surrounding area.

Finally two EMTs manipulated the uncooperative corpse into a black vinyl body bag.

When the small, stunned crowd eventually dispersed, Becky and Andy turned to walk home, taking the conventional route along Bailey Road.

Today, there'd be no shortcut through the natural habitat surrounding the popular pond.

CHAPTER NINE

"Geez, Becky, I...I never saw a dead body before in my life! And look who the hell it turns out to be. It's our own mystery dude from Hook Island, Jack the biker. Man, he must have pissed somebody off in some big freakin' way. Did you see the size of the gunshot hole in his head?"

The two walked slowly, still stunned by the event at Peck's Pond.

"Yeah...but I...I can't imagine what the hell went on. I never saw a dead body before either. And now we see one who wasn't just dead but has been freakin' murdered! And we...we recognized the poor guy on top of that."

Andy turned to look at her as they walked along and said, "This is like some creepy mystery we're watching on TV. But...but it's real this time."

"Andy, I feel a little freaked out with all this. We both know that this...this Jack something or other, was murdered on Peck's Pond. But his friend or...or partner of some sorts and our teacher, Miss Lakely, still has no idea what happened. She only knows the police and fire trucks pulled up over here with sirens blaring. We left her in the classroom thinking there was just a grass fire started by some kids smoking."

For several minutes there was silence between them. Andy finally spoke.

"Beck, do…do you think they were ah, you know, a couple or something? Do you think Miss Lakely and this dead biker dude had been seeing each other?"

Becky didn't respond. She only stared at her friend as they waited for the crosswalk light to change.

"I have no idea what their relationship is, or…or was. But we do know they knew each other and were involved with something that took place at Hook Island. And Jack was also at the parking lot after the graduation ceremony."

"What do you think they'll do with his body? I mean, what'll they do before it is claimed?"

"I'm sure the cops need to have an autopsy done to develop some leads on suspects. The Forensics Department will have to see what they discover going over his body with a fine-toothed comb. And, they have to identify the victim and notify his next of kin." Becky looked over to her friend. "C'mon, Andy, haven't you ever watched *Law and Order* or *CSI*?"

"Yeah, yeah, I guess. But, geez, I just can't believe this murder happened right across the street from our own high school. And on top of that, you and I know a little about the poor dude. I'm sure none of the other kids know him. And, they certainly don't know he has a connection to one of our teachers."

"Yeah, but remember, you and I aren't supposed to know anything about him and his being with Miss Lakely on Hook Island. We were illegally spying on them on property that had 'No Trespassing" signs all over it. And, if we tell our story to the police or anyone else, we'll incriminate ourselves and have to implicate our teacher."

"Geez, Becky, sometimes, I swear, you sound like a lawyer. Is law school in your future or what?"

She chuckled.

"No way! But I do think Miss Lakely will be brought into this case sooner or later. And you know she'll keep it private since their relationship, whatever it is, is personal and confidential. But, you know, I wonder if somebody else has seen the two of them together. As soon as she comes forward and reveals her relationship with him, pieces to this puzzle will start to fit together."

The mid-day temperature was rising again, promising another hot, humid, summer scorcher in southeastern Connecticut. The two teenagers soon approached their Beechwood Knoll neighborhood.

"Andy, I think we have to get all this crap out of our heads. After all, we aren't directly involved and we'll let the police do their job and see what happens. Say, do you want to go to the beach this afternoon? I haven't been there yet this summer, and it's a perfect day for a swim."

"Yeah, sounds cool! How about biking down to my house after lunch! And, maybe later we can work on our Logic homework assignment. It can't be too difficult. I already know what a paradox is."

"Sounds like a plan."

Wollaston Beach, located about a half mile east of Beechwood Knoll's upscale neighborhood, was crowed on this hot, hazy, summer day. Families were now spending the summer vacation with toddlers at the shore. Colorful beach umbrellas, ice coolers, playpens, and other children's beach toys dotted the sandy stretch along Wollaston Boulevard. A variety of odors mixed in with salty air. The unmistakable scent of coconut oil blended with tanning cream seemed to come from every beach blanket and folding chair. The tantalizing smell of grilled hot dogs and sausages wafted from the vendors who were strategically spaced apart in the packed parking lot.

One section of the sandy beach was traditionally claimed by the high school kids. Today there were more than thirty teenagers lying on blankets close together. They all relaxed, talking, listening to their music, and just chilling out. The section claimed by the high school students was traditionally off limits to any adult invasion.

Becky unfolded a blanket near the group. Andy helped, stretching it out and anchoring it down with some of their belongings.

They said hello to some of their friends passing by, tiptoeing in between some of the other blankets. They all knew one another from classes, sports, or band.

Andy stripped off his jersey to expose his pale, white body in contrast to his colorful, knee-length "Bahama Joe" bathing suit.

Becky slowly peeled off her top, folding it neatly and placing it on the blanket. She then wiggled out of her denim shorts, now showing off her hot-pink bikini bathing suit. The vibrant suit contrasted nicely with her naturally golden-hued skin. The skimpy style also emphasized her fit body with her maturing soft curves.

The teenagers had multiple conversations going on about latest gossip about who was going out with whom, the best parties coming up, movies, and other celebrity news. There was some subdued buzz about the DUI of Cindy Shea resulting in her tragic death. Suddenly, one of the boys yelled out, "Hey, did you guys hear about the body they pulled out of Peck's Pond this morning? The poor bastard was murdered! He was shot dead—a bullet hole right in his freakin' head!"

The young man's announcement energized the group with speculation about who the victim might have been and what he was doing in Peck's Park. The rumors quickly percolated that the murder was probably related to a drug deal gone bad.

But a homicide in the quiet little town of North Haven vibrated the gossip around the blankets for several minutes.

Becky and Andy intentionally stayed out of the conversations. Andy stood up and reached for Becky's hand to help her up from their blanket. They quietly strolled down to the wavy water lapping at the shoreline. After stopping at the water's edge, they hesitated at the thought of the cold saltwater on their heated bodies. Still, giggling with anticipation, they agreed to take one quick running plunge together into the surf.

They quickly ran into the water until nearly waist deep then surface-dived into the next wave coming at them. The two then playfully engaged in a game of splashing and frolicking in the chilly but refreshing ocean water. Later, Becky convinced Andy to let her climb up onto his shoulders so she could jump into the waves. She made the jump quickly before his thin frame weakened from her added weight.

They were having fun, and when they stopped with their antics, Andy came closer to Becky bobbing in the wavy water. He now had a more serious expression on his face.

"Why the sad face all of a sudden?" she asked him.

"Oh, it's just a little problem that I'm trying to figure out."

Becky stopped bobbing up and down. She anchored her feet into the underwater sand and looked up into Andy's deep, blue eyes that now had a pink tint from the mild stinging of the salty water.

"I bet you're still thinking about Jack the biker, aren't you?"

"No, no that's not it," he replied, shaking his head gently. "Actually it's kind of a personal problem that I've been struggling with these past few weeks."

"So, tell me what it is, if it's not too personal."

"It's okay. I'll try to explain. It's actually a little weird. See, I'm supposed to sign up for football tryouts tomorrow and also visit my doctor for a physical exam so I can be eligible."

"Hmm. I didn't know you played football," she commented, trying to visualize her slender friend suited up in a football uniform. "So what's the problem with that? Do you think you'll flunk the doctor's exam?"

"No, no. See, the real problem is I…I don't really think I want to try out for the team. In fact *I know* I don't want to try out for the team. First of all, I'm not strong enough, and second, I'm really not into the game of football. But...see, my older brother was a big star when he played for North Haven a few years ago. And my father expects me to at least try out. He thinks I'd make a great wide-receiver with my height. But my heart and...and frankly, my stomach, aren't really into it. And, if I don't at least go for the tryouts, my dad will be really disappointed. On the other hand, I'm not my brother. In fact my older brother and I have little in common. He's always been a jock and I'd rather do more...you know, academic things. I like to explore, to learn, to expand intellectually. Besides, I like being on the marching band and if I ever did make the team, I'd have to give that up. But my dad puts more value on his sons being athletes than band members."

"Hmm, I see the problem."

He paused then looked directly into Becky's eyes. "The reason I'm telling you is this is what has been on my mind besides all the other stuff going on at Hook Island, et cetera, et cetera."

Becky dog-paddled herself over very close to where Andy stood. "Then, don't do it. I've met your dad a couple of times. I think he's a pretty cool guy. Let him know exactly how you feel about football and just...just be honest with him."

"Yeah, I mean I love all sports, and he wants me to compete, but I'm not into physical competition. It's just not my thing. I'd much rather be figuring out mathematical equations than getting my head crushed."

"I know, I know," she grinned.

Becky stared up at her friend, sensing his dilemma. But she was now more struck with him sharing a very personal emotional problem with her. She knew Andy was unlike most young men. He was more mature than most boys his age and not trapped in a superficial ego.

Her thoughts suddenly spawned an idea.

"Hey, if your dad wants you to go out for sports, you can still do that. But it doesn't have to be football! Why don't you go out for the golf team? Both the girls' team and the boys' team lost a lot of seniors with this year's graduating class. So, there'll be lots of opportunities to get an opened spot. I was going to look into it myself. And I remember you once telling me that you played golf before, right?"

"Yeah, well, I went out on the course with Bumper quite a bit and caddied for my dad a few times. I liked it, actually, and was beginning to improve."

"And if we played on the school golf teams we could still play with the marching band."

"Boy, I'm not sure if I'm good enough to make the golf team," Andy said.

"Well, I've been playing a lot of golf for two years now. I tell you what! Let's go to the driving range tonight. I can give you some pointers I've picked up from my own lessons. Then we can plan on signing up for the team this September."

Andy looked again into the soft, coal-black eyes of his cute friend.

"Geez, I don't know if my dad will go for that. He still has fond memories of my older brother suited up in a football uniform."

"Well, if golf doesn't make him happy, just tell him you can't leave the school's marching band to be on the football team."

Andy chuckled at her attempt to help him out.

"Ha, he knows there are plenty of coronet players to fill my spot on the school band."

Becky paused then said, "Okay, so then you just got to tell him the truth."

"Tell him the truth?"

"Yeah, you can't leave the band to play football because you'll miss being with me, your new girlfriend. He's gotta understand that, right?"

They both giggled then flirted playfully as they splashed water on each other. As a result of her teasing remark, Andy suddenly gained a new measure of confidence. With many of their friends around them, he expanded his bare chest with pride. He was with a cute girl with a great personality that matched her attractive figure in her pink bikini. They walked out of the water with Andy grabbing her hand in his. They slowly walked upon the sandy beach toward the exclusive site of teenage blankets.

"Hey Becky, your speaking of the girls' golf team reminded me of something. I had an interesting talk with Tyler Farnham this morning about our quiet classmate, Amber Woods."

Andy told Becky what he had learned about the shy and attractive senior. He disclosed Tyler's surprise at how the young woman had morphed from an outgoing popular student into a quasi-hermit.

"Hmm, I wonder what happened to make her change her personality all of a sudden."

"Tyler said he had no clue, but whatever it was happened during our April vacation. He could pinpoint it to that spring break week when she went through some kinda strange transformation."

"Hmm. That is really weird. I've never spoken with Amber, not even in the bathroom. She is just so quiet."

The two dropped the subject and spent the rest of the afternoon lying on their blanket, soaking up the sun and munching on snacks. With ear buds inserted, they listened to their iPods and chatted with friends. The only interruption was a cell phone call Andy received from Bumper, still in New York City.

After disconnecting, he rolled over and updated his blanket mate.

"Well, that was kinda sad. Bumper just told me his grandfather died yesterday. The funeral is tomorrow. He told me he's gonna stay with his mother down there in New York for a while afterwards. They have to clear out the apartment and all that stuff."

"Oh...that's too bad. How's he handling everything?"

"Okay, it seems. He feels bad for his mom and wants to stay and support her. He also told me he's found some new, as he calls them, 'summer friends.'

Evidently he likes the New York *scene*...as he put it. He'll contact me in a couple of days."

"Huh! Little does he know what's going on up here! And how we are involved with because...because of his dumb freakin' idea to snoop out on Hook Island. If it wasn't for him, we'd never know this Jack the biker dude, or discover that Miss Lakely's involved with something that's just...just...I don't know, bizarre."

"Yeah, it's typical of Bumper to start something and not follow through with it."

"Like his diets?" Becky asked, jokingly.

* * *

That evening, Mrs. Bing drove the two teens to the Seaside Driving Range. The popular practice spot was located not far from their affluent neighborhood. At the entrance to the range, Becky pulled her golf bag full of clubs out from the back of the SUV.

When they arrived inside the Seaside Pro Shack, she told Andy which clubs to select to begin his first lesson.

As the summer twilight sky faded to black, the two continued swinging at golf balls under the stadium-styled, overhead lights. She gave Andy some basic lessons on the mechanics of the golf swing and the importance of a good comfortable hand grip on the club. After a while he seemed to get it and was soon hitting the ball straight and high up into the air.

After depleting the large bucket of golf balls, they left the driving range and walked along the town sidewalk headed for the nearby Dunkin' Donuts. Andy carried Becky's clubs, making a joke about being her "subservient caddy."

They sat at a small table inside the coffee shop. Andy ordered a Raspberry Coolatta. Becky selected a vanilla Chai Tea. Their discussion skirted around plans to play a round of golf together on an 18-hole course as soon as they could. But the conversation quickly segued into other germane activities.

"Hey, Beck, I've been meaning to ask you. Did you notice a weird difference with Miss Lakely this morning in class? It keeps coming back to me. I mean, did she look a little different to you today?"

Becky took a quiet slurp from her drink.

"Yeah, I think all us kids noticed the change in her. She just wasn't herself today. And she just never got into the subject as she usually does."

"I know. But...but what did you think about her looks?"

"Well, she looked like she was kinda tired, and a little pale. But maybe she was just having a bad day." Becky paused then looked straight into her friend's eyes. "You know, Andy, women *are entitled* to have a bad day—every once in a while."

Andy backed away from her slightly and stared at her for a moment without saying a word. It was clear he got the message laced with a stinging feminine tone.

After finishing their drinks, they stepped outside to begin the walk home. They resumed their conversation walking along the sidewalk lit with the town streetlamps.

"Yeah, but I disagree, Beck. I don't think Miss Lakely just had a *bad day*. You see, I think she had had a *bad night* before class today. And, I wonder if she had the same bad night that Jack the biker experienced just before being shot to death!"

Andy carried Becky's golf bag over his shoulder as they walked quietly toward Beechwood Knoll. Neither of them wanted to articulate a theory that was revving up in their minds. Right now, everything was pure speculation but they silently wondered if Miss Lakely had been with the mysterious biker on the night he was murdered.

Much of the remainder of the walk home was in silence. As they approached Beechwood Knoll, Becky offered her own summary of the mysterious case.

"I think we'll find out more tonight on the eleven o'clock news. If...if it was a drug deal that went bad, the police will certainly report that. Plus, maybe we'll learn Jack's full name. But we may or may not find out what Miss Lakely was doing with him the other day at Hook. And, we may never find out who she spoke with on her cell phone after he had left that creepy, cruddy, underground office."

Andy walked Becky to her front door then slipped of her golf bag from his shoulder and handed it to her. He smiled at her, then said, "Hey, thanks for helping me with my homework tonight!"

"Your homework? Andy, what the hell are you talking about? I helped you with some tips on your golf swing."

"Ah, but I don't think so. You taught me in order to strike the golf ball so it *goes up high* into the air I need to *swing down* on the ball. And, if I want the ball to go a long distance quickly, I shouldn't swing fast, but should swing more slowly and deliberate. See, Becky, these are each good examples of a paradox. And that was what we had for the homework assignment. Don't you remember? Miss Lakely asked us to think about and identify things that are the opposite of what we believe to be true."

Becky burst out laughing.

"Oh my God, Andy! You're such an incredible nerdy, wise ass!" She laughed loudly and then gently pushed Andy away from her and off the porch steps.

"Good Night, Andy!"

"Night, Becky!" the young man said, walking away with a big smile on his face.

CHAPTER TEN

Upon arriving home, Andy spent some time chatting with his parents. He recounted his version of what he and the other students had seen earlier in the day. He described the police and firemen removing the dead body out of Peck's Pond.

Alarmed at the news, the Abbots had many questions that Andy fielded without revealing his personal recognition of the murdered victim.

After they had covered the sensational story, Andy changed topics and told his parents how he enjoyed his informal golf lesson with Becky Bing. His enthusiasm and energy signaled to them his interest in picking it up as a school sport. It was the perfect opportunity for Andy to announce he was pursing golf as his sport of choice and not varsity football.

He immediately sensed that both of his parents were happy with his decision. Seeing that his dad wasn't disappointed, Andy felt relief as an emotional weight came off of him. The three Abbots agreed to go out together during the summer vacation to play some golf at the local country club course.

"Oh, and if we all play at your country club, Dad, can I invite Becky to join us and make a foursome?"

Mr. Abbot smiled and glanced over at his grinning wife.

"Of course, invite Becky anytime."

"We're just staying up for the eleven o'clock news, Andy. Do you want to stay down here with us?"

"No, no thanks, I think I'll catch it upstairs on my bedroom TV. I'm pretty beat now, anyway."

He left them and skipped upstairs. As he stripped down for bed, he turned on his own bedroom TV.

The young brunette newscaster opened the program with:

"The town of North Haven was shocked today when Police Detectives reported finding an unidentified body in the Peck's Park area, across the street from North Haven High School.

"The victim had been shot in the middle of the forehead. His body had been submerged in the swampy Peck's Pond and had to be pulled out by an NHFD underwater diver."

There was a brief video clip taken at the crime scene before the anchorwoman continued with her report.

"The North Haven Police provided no further information pending an in-depth investigation. After identification, they'll notify next of kin before releasing the name of the murder victim to the public. Ron Souza, Chief of Detectives, told reporters he'd hold a press conference later in the week with more detailed information about the case.

"This homicide is only the third in the town of North Haven in the past forty years."

As soon as Andy slid under the bedcovers he heard a text message alert on his cell. He reached over and saw it was from Becky.

"did u c TV late news?" she wrote.

"yeah! what do u think?"

"right now, we know more about the 'vic' than cops do. at least we know his name is JACK."

"yeah, I don't feel good about this. do u think they'll ask Miss L questions?"

"don't know, but truth will come out soon."

"yeah, I just hope it wasn't over drugs."

"good night, Andy."

"good night, Becky... Thx for golf lesson."

Andy closed his eyes in the darkened room. He first meditated on how grateful he was with his parents' reaction. He was happy he didn't hurt his dad's feelings. With that issue off his mind, he began thinking about his newest and best friend. His closed eyes let him fantasize an image of his cute companion with her alluring dimpled smile. The mental vision of Becky's smiling face relaxed his body before he drifted off into a deep and satisfying sleep.

* * *

The next morning's Internet edition of the *New Haven Register* printed the story of the shocking murder in the neighboring town of North Haven. The headlines were in bold text—**Murder at the Pond!** But there were no additional details of the story than those already presented in the TV newscast.

However, the story emphasized that since there were no suspects yet in the murder, the killer could still be walking around the town's streets and surrounding area. The only quote came from Chief of Police Souza who underscored how his staff would be working 24/7 to find the person or persons responsible for the homicide. The fact that the victim's body was found directly across the street from the town's high school with summer school students inside added another level of community concern and urgency.

As the students arrived for classes the next day, they still buzzed about the murdered man fished out of Peck's Pond.

As each of the five students crossed the threshold of Room 205 into the AP Intro to Logic course, they were met with a surprise.

Miss Lakely wasn't sitting at her desk. Instead, there was someone else, who was also familiar to them, seated in the chair behind the teacher's desk. His closed-lips grin was unmistakable as each of the students quietly took their seats.

The middle-aged man was not a stranger to them. Dressed in one of his typical expensive suits topping glossy-black, patent leather shoes, the principal of the high school, Mr. Al Pratt, stood up and stepped toward the front line of students' desks.

"Students, I'm sorry to inform you that Miss Lakely won't be in class today. Nor will she be in for the rest of this week. She had a…a…ah, some personal emergency that took her out of town. So, I will conduct summer class today the best I can. I did, ah…speak with Miss Lakely last evening and she gave me your independent work assignment for the remainder of this week.

"Now, I'll be honest, I am *not* a Logic expert. But I do remember a few things about the Introduction to Logic in some of my college Philosophy courses. So, we can perhaps have a brief group discussion as Amanda…ah, Miss Lakely, usually did with you. After that, you may either stay here at school to work on your independent project, or leave to work on it at home."

The next half hour was spent reviewing the process of deductive and inductive reasoning. It was a flat and dull thirty minutes. The next segment of the class was spent with each student discussing and giving examples of paradoxes. Each had to provide how paradoxes must be considered when performing good logical analysis. Although the students were prepared, the morning class session dragged on. With Mr. Pratt as the class leader, the period was lifeless and awkward at best, with many quiet pauses.

The principal then read aloud from a notepad. It was the outline of their advanced homework project that was to be turned in before the last day of class.

The assignment, provided to him by Miss Lakely, was to reference internet websites to learn about flow diagrams, decision trees, and "if, then, else" models in logical software programming. The remainder of the project required each of them to develop their own logic diagram to solve a hypothetical problem or puzzle.

"So, are there any questions for me before you are dismissed for today?" Mr. Pratt asked the class.

Hans Schmidt raised his hand.

"Is...is Miss Lakely going to be coming back?"

A disturbing expression washed over the principal's face.

"Oh, Hans, yes, yes, of course! Miss Lakely, she, ah...had some ah...she told me she had a personal issue to take care of back in Chicago. She plans to be back here next Monday morning. So, we really need not have formal classes unless you choose to do so. Therefore, it seems you'll get a couple of extra days off and more time to work on your independent homework assignment."

Mr. Pratt's face contorted into his trademark grin. The sly and superficial smile did nothing to change the lackluster mood among the students.

"Now, before dismissal, I want to change topics. I have an administrative favor to ask of each of you. One of our office secretaries, Mrs. Lynch, suddenly had to take a leave of absence and will be out for the remainder of the summer. And my personal secretary, Marie, ah...Mrs. Savoyski, will be taking some well-earned time off she had planned. So, I'd like to ask that any of you, or all of you, consider pitching in part-time to help out a few hours in the office, if you can. Your hours can be flexible, and you'll be paid a very good hourly wage. Most of the work is filing, sending out mailings, and some administrative computer work. Of course, I personally might have some special tasks for you to work on from time to time."

"Ah, when do you need the extra help in the office, Mr. Pratt?" Hans asked.

"Oh, I could use someone as early as next week. It might be for a couple of hours a day, and as I said, we can work out flexible schedules to make it easy and not ruin your summer vacation. Just stop by the office and let Mrs. Savoyski know if you're interested. And, your work time will be documented and placed into your personal achievement records. I'm sure you all know that colleges and universities are always interested in extra-curricular experience—even if it's administrative in nature."

With little reaction, the teens stood up quietly saying goodbye to the grinning Mr. Pratt and then filed past him to leave the classroom. It was the coy smile and his thick, shiny, grey hair that gave him the nickname "the silver fox," a moniker that stuck with him year after year.

After Becky and Andy walked briskly out of the school building and crossed onto Bailey Road, they caught sight of Amber Woods strolling slowly on the cement sidewalk. She walked in front of them, staring into nothingness as if she were in some hypnotic daze.

Spontaneously and uncharacteristically, Becky shouted out to the zombie-like Amber.

"Hey Amber, wait up! I need to ask you something about the girls' golf team!"

The attractive senior stopped. She turned to face Becky who was walking briskly with Andy following behind her.

Amber was surprised by the question and taken out of her personal space, as Becky stopped within inches of her.

"Huh? Oh...ah sure, what...what is it, Becky? Oh, the school golf team? I played for the past couple of years but...but I won't be playing again this year. What...what's on your mind?"

They both turned and continued walking in the same direction. Andy remained quiet just a few feet behind them.

"Actually, both Andy here and I are going out for the golf teams this coming fall for the first time. And, ah...I was just, you know, interested in how you liked it and what...you know, what the competition is like."

Becky kept eye contact with the pretty blonde as she spoke, pleased with her own questions. Andy moved up to Becky's side, with them now walking three abreast along the sidewalk.

"Well, I…can't speak for the boys' team, Andy," Amber answered, looking toward the tall young man, "but we do play the same schools on the same dates. That's so we can all travel together on one bus to the golf matches. But…but what exactly did you want to know?"

As Becky listened, she was mentally searching for her follow-up question, intent on learning more about this quiet, mysterious upperclassman. The three of them waited for the traffic light to change, which would enable the trio to cross Washington Avenue, the commercial backbone of North Haven.

"Oh, well, for one thing, I didn't know what kind of handicap would be good enough to make the team. I've played a few years and hope I'm good enough to make the team but my handicap is still kinda high; about a 15. So, just how good are the others on the North Haven team and the competition from the other schools?"

"I guess overall for the team, a solid eighteen-hole handicap is usually between say….twelve and twenty. But if it's a little higher, that's okay. You must know that we play only nine-hole matches with the other schools. But for the regional playoffs we have eighteen-hole matches."

"I see. And, um, what about the golf practice sessions? I mean, Andy and I just started this season with hitting some balls at the driving range. But we intend on getting out to a golf course real soon. How often did you play each week to get tuned up for the school's team?"

Amber's lips curled into a grin for the first time which she followed with a slight chuckle. The subtle smile lit up her face and made her look even more beautiful. It was no wonder she was considered the prettiest girl in the class. And it was obvious she could easily garner any modeling or acting career in her future with her physical attributes alone.

"Well, I'm kinda fortunate in the practicing category. In the beginning of the season, the team practiced a couple of times a week at the local course. But in my case, I got a lot of practice in on my own. See, my dad works as the greens keeper at the Yale Golf Course in New Haven. And because of that, I can get on the course almost anytime I want. After I got my license to drive I was there nearly every day last summer. So, to answer your question, I was playing *at least* four or five times a week. That's how I brought my handicap down and learned to play better. I actually went out on the course solo a lot of times when it wasn't busy. But I also learned from others who I got grouped up with to make up a threesome or foursome."

The young woman then went on to describe how the golf team matches were held, the team camaraderie, and the ethics-building inherent in the game.

Andy was surprised as he witnessed the heretofore unveiled and pleasant persona of this young woman. It wasn't just the energy of her natural beauty, but how she spoke so confidently and articulately. She was clearly intelligent and talented and at the same time never condescending to the two of them. When she spoke of her golf experience she held direct eye contact.

The three continued walking along with Becky asking about the golf course, the team coach, and which girls Amber expected to return in the fall.

As they walked, Andy simply listened, not knowing where Becky was going with all of this talk. *Was she really trying to find out about the golf team, or did she just want to find out more about the quiet and reserved Amber Woods?*

After Amber seemed a little more relaxed, Becky switched topics as they ambled along the paved sidewalk.

"Geez, this morning's class really sucked, didn't it? I mean that Mr. Pratt sure as hell is no Miss Lakely!"

"Humph," Amber replied, her expression suddenly turning sour. She immediately turned away from the two juniors.

Oh shit! I just hit a freakin' nerve, Becky thought to herself.

It was a definite hot button as the young blonde appeared to close up tighter than a clam shell. It was obvious Amber did not want to talk about anything but golf with her classmates. But Becky wouldn't or couldn't let it go.

"So, I was interested in the offer to work in the office a few hours a week. I might just stop by and look into working there this summer. But first I..."

Amber stopped walking. Her complexion suddenly turned to a crimson color and her eyes squinted.

"Becky, whatever the fuck you do, *don't*...I mean *don't* work in that school office! Please don't do it! For your own sake! You'll regret you ever made that decision!"

Shocked at the explosive reaction, Andy stumbled over his own feet, nearly falling face down before he awkwardly caught his balance. Neither he nor Becky had anticipated such a sudden change in tone and language.

Becky backed off as they continued walking in uncomfortable silence. She knew it was time to chill a little.

"Say, I could go for a coffee or cold drink. Can I buy you one, Amber? You've been so helpful to me today telling me all about the golf thing!"

"Ah, no, no. I gotta run. I'm...I'm late already."

With that, Becky and Andy stopped while Amber walked briskly away from them. The abrupt departure left the two standing on the sidewalk, dumbfounded at the transformed social interaction.

"Oh, thanks, Amber! I really appreciated it!" Becky shouted out to her as she walked off into the distance. But Amber didn't respond verbally. She simply kept walking with her head down then offered a quick, halfhearted wave in the air without turning around.

Becky and Andy changed direction and headed home toward Beechwood Knoll.

"Oh my God! What the hell just happened?" Andy asked.

"Geez, I sure as hell don't know but I hope I didn't upset her. She did seem to come apart there at the end, didn't she?"

Andy paused for a moment before responding.

"Well, she said she was already late for something. Maybe that was on her mind and she just wanted to end the conversation and move on so she could get to her destination quickly."

Becky shot Andy a disappointed look. Her voice reflected it too.

"C'mon, Andy! Think about it! What the hell was she really late for? She wasn't late for anything! We got dismissed over an hour early from today's class. She didn't know that Miss Lakely was going to be absent today and we'd get let go from class so early. She, like the rest of us, should still be sitting in the classroom right now. Telling us she was late was just a line of BS and her way of quickly getting rid of us!"

Andy walked quietly along, knowing his friend's analysis was right.

"I guess I was just trying to give her the benefit of the doubt. She seemed so nice and friendly at first. And I enjoyed listening to her especially…especially since she…"

Becky shot a stare at her companion, interrupting him mid-sentence.

"Since what? Since she is so *hot-looking*?"

"No, no! I wasn't going to say that. I was going to say….since she's a senior—an upperclassman."

The duo walked along without any further dialogue. But Andy suppressed a private grin celebrating his minor victory. For the first time, Becky had displayed jealousy over his interest in another girl.

When they passed by the entrance to Peck Park guarding the now infamous pond, neither of them would turn their heads to peer over at the crime scene.

Later, while approaching their Beechwood Knoll neighborhood, Andy thought about Hook Island once again.

"Hey, Beck, I just thought of something! Do you know what we never did? We never checked out that video I took on my camcorder of New Age. Do you want to check it out with me at my house?"

"Yeah, sure, that's cool!"

Andy's mother greeted the two of them at the door to a long, screened, front porch. It was an old-fashioned styled, farmer's porch with small tables and rocking chairs placed on the deck.

"Hi, Mom! You remember Becky Bing. "

"Yes, of course, it's good to see you again," answered the slightly overweight, middle-aged woman with temples showing grey. "You sure are home early from school today! Was there a problem with the crime across the street?"

"No, Mrs. Abbot," Becky answered. "We just got dismissed early today." She then explained how Miss Lakely was out that day, and that the principal had filled in and given them their take home assignment.

"Hey, Mom, we're going upstairs to my room to work on our class project. Even though we don't have classes for a couple of days, without a substitute teacher, we still have to work on it."

"Sure! Help yourself to some cold drinks and a snack in the kitchen. I'm going to be weeding out in the garden for a while."

Becky followed Andy up the wooden staircase, down a hallway, and into his bedroom. She had never been inside the Abbot home before. Her eyes panned the walls to see posters from the movie "The Transformers" and some professional athlete action photos. She was amused to notice he had the same oversized photo of Albert Einstein, pictured with his unruly rush of grey hair and curious expression that could be interpreted in so many ways.

Andy grabbed his new Sony camcorder from a shelf then connected it to his bedroom TV. The video was of good quality despite the dimly lit underground factory.

They watched silently at the close-up shots of the performers. The groupie friends in the small audience could be clearly seen sitting close to the makeshift stage.

As they watched the video unfold on the small TV screen, they relived that frightening night on the island. The scenes brought back memories of peering in the factory window, the thunderstorm, and the police raid, culminating with their dangerous swim across Hook River to escape being arrested.

They sat close together on Andy's bed, glued to the TV screen, listening to the music. The police megaphone suddenly blurted out commands to the trespassers, once again making the teens flinch with fear. The next images from the camera were difficult to look at. The camera caught only blurred images as it quickly tumbled down from Andy's hand. Then the screen faded to black as the camcorder lens became buried in the pile of old fabric.

Andy stood up to turn off the TV and disconnect the cables. Before he did so, Becky spoke quickly.

"Hey, before you disconnect, can you rewind to about mid-way into the video. I thought I saw something moving in the background. But I have no idea what the heck it was."

He grabbed the remote control and alternately rewound and forwarded the digital video recording several times.

"Wait, wait, stop it right there!" Becky said.

Andy then altered the speed of the video to slow motion. The two stared at the screen.

"There, there it is, Andy. Did you see it?"

"Huh, what are you talking about?"

"Rewind again, just a bit. And go super slow, like you know, frame by frame. Keep your eye on the dark background beyond the audience. Look for a tiny bright light moving around. The groupies in the audience are focused on watching the band perform. They are either totally disinterested or don't seem to see the little moving light."

Andy repositioned the images and kept viewing it in slow motion. Then he saw it.

"Yeah, I see it! It seems to jerk around in some kind of random, weird moves. Maybe it's one of those mini-flashlights or one of those high intensity lights that cops use."

"Yeah, but I bet it's not a cop holding that tiny light. Remember the cruisers hadn't even come onto the scene yet."

"I just wonder if it's something mechanical with a light source on it. Maybe it's some kinda small machine or motor or something, you know, with an LED on it."

"Let's look at the whole thing from the beginning of this segment and just focus on that dark section of the factory."

They rearranged their positions on the bed, now lying side by side on their stomachs. Their cupped hands and folded elbows supported their chins as they focused on the screen.

Once again, they saw the tiny light on the screen, surrounded completely by the factory's darkness. Not one person in the seated audience seemed distracted by the jumping, pinpoint light. The bright, tiny circle jerked in irregular movements, stopped for a moment, then moved around in irregular patterns once again.

"Becky, I have no clue what the hell that light is. I just can't imagine someone from the audience standing in the darkness by himself, jerking a mini-flashlight around."

"Yeah. But I'm not so much intrigued by the light itself, but more interested in who might be holding that light."

"Oh, that's gonna be tough. There's not a helluva lot of light in that rear section of the factory. My camera is good, but for something like this you'd need a night camera, you know, one with an infrared feature."

"I know, but wait! I just got an idea. If we can download some of these video image frames from your camcorder to a computer, we can then download them to a portable memory stick."

"Yeah, so what does that buy us?"

"Well, it so happens my dad has some new software on his computer at home. It's an image enhancement program to zoom in on anatomy sections. He got it to do his research work for the Yale School of Medicine. The software can greatly enhance digital image files. It enables people to see things that cannot be seen with the naked eye. It blows up the image and you can embellish the frame by stripping away any obstructions."

"Hmm. Well, I can easily download the images to my computer. And I can just as easily transfer them onto a flash drive or burn a CD. So, when can we get access to your dad's software?"

"How about we do it some night this week? My father's away for a week at a medical conference so his study will be free. Come over to my house after dinner and we can load the files onto his computer."

"Great! But I have to ask you something. Can you stay here for lunch? We can make sandwiches and eat out the patio."

"Sure. I'll call my mom and let her know. She'll be expecting me home pretty soon."

Downstairs inside the kitchen, Mrs. Abbot joined Becky and Andy at the kitchen table as they made and ate tuna salad sandwiches, chips, and soda. After chatting for a while, Andy's mom left them alone to resume her weeding and pruning in the backyard garden. Once his mother was out of earshot, and as they were rinsing off their plates at the kitchen sink, Andy leaned down toward Becky with a question in a near whisper.

"Hey, Becky, I don't want you to get all pissed off, but what do you make of our walk this morning with Amber? I mean, I know she dumped us after a while, but what do you make of her warning us not to work in the office?"

Becky's eyes swiveled over to her friend.

"I really don't know but I've been thinking about it, too. When Amber and I talked about the golf team at first, she was so cool. But when I brought up about working part-time in the school's office, I freakin' pressed a really hot button for her. Oh my God, she went nuts!"

"I…I just didn't get it. Why the hell would she say *you'd regret it* if you worked in the office?"

"I haven't a clue. Maybe she meant the office job isn't worth the pay and it's boring." Becky knew how naïve her theory sounded. She quickly recovered with a follow-up supposition. "Or perhaps, there's something weird going on in the office she didn't want us to get involved with."

Andy looked at Becky curiously. "Weird?"

"I don't know. But we do know one thing," Becky continued.

"What's that?"

"You and I are gonna find out."

"Find out? How the hell are we going to find out?"

"We'll explore after you and I volunteer to work part-time in the office next Monday morning."

Andy was about to protest, but thought better and changed his mind. He kept his mouth shut and simply smiled at his cute and determined friend.

CHAPTER ELEVEN

Before heading out of the house to return home, Becky skipped upstairs and into Andy's bedroom to get her Coach shoulder bag she'd left on top of his bed. When she stepped inside the room she noticed that the TV was still on. As she grabbed her bag and turned to head back downstairs, she noticed that a news segment showed the North Haven Police Chief preparing to speak to the media.

"Hey, Andy, c'mon upstairs! Hurry up!"

The two sat on his bed with their eyes once again riveted to the flat TV screen.

The news station's camera zoomed in on Chief Souza who introduced himself to the surrounding reporters. He adjusted the microphone at the podium and looked out into the crowd of journalists.

"I want to give you an update on the body found at Peck's Park across from North Haven High School yesterday. After I give me my briefing I will answer any questions you might have. But I must remind you that the case is still in the early stages of investigation and some information may not be forthcoming to protect the interests involved.

"At approximately nine-fifteen yesterday morning, a call was received at the North Haven Police station. The anonymous caller reported that a dead body was located in Peck's Pond. There was no further information and the caller immediately hung up. We attempted to identify the person who made the call but the source was untraceable.

"With two cruisers immediately sent to the scene, there was no sign of a body or anyone else in the area. But the Fire Rescue Unit's underwater diver explored Peck's Pond and soon discovered the aforementioned body.

"This SCUBA diver pulled out a white male approximately thirty years of age. He had long, black, shoulder-length hair. The victim had a muscular build with both arms covered with intricate tattoos. But for now, the victim is still unidentified. We are asking anyone who might know or has seen anyone meeting that description, to call the North Haven Police as soon as possible.

"The cause of death was a single bullet shot through the skull into the middle of the forehead. The weapon used for the shooting was a Glock nine-millimeter handgun. Early indications are that the gun was fired from a close range.

"Currently, the medical forensic people are performing the detailed autopsy and we look for a report from that department within seventy-two hours. And, that's all I have to report for now."

The media mavens were quick to fire off questions:

"Chief, is there any concern for the immediate safety of the students with the murder taking place so close to the high school?"

"We're always concerned for our children, but this crime appears to have nothing to do with the students. Right now, there is no immediate concern.

"Was the murder committed at Peck's Pond?"

"At this time, we believe it wasn't, but we're still working on that. We believe the murder may have taken place elsewhere and the victim's body was dragged to Peck's Pond and subsequently dumped into the water."

"Do you have a time of death?"

"We have to wait for the autopsy to confirm that."

After the questions, Chief Souza spoke again.

"I will schedule another press conference after we learn more about this case. We will provide you with more information available at that time. And as always, we encourage anyone who might know anything about this crime to call us at our police headquarters."

Regular TV programming resumed and Andy looked at Becky.

"Geez, Becky, this is really weird! Now I feel we should go to the police and tell them what we know. I mean, at least we can tell them we know the victim's first name is Jack and that he was at the Hook Island factories before he was killed."

"And, ah, excuse me. You want to do this, why? Should we tell them that we're guilty of trespassing then we'll tell them we're also guilty of breaking and entering and all that crap? Or do you mean to tell me you want to go to the police, turn ourselves in, and tell them our story about our teacher and Jack as in *doing our civic duty*?"

Andy now looked sheepish, realizing how they had changed roles. He quickly reversed direction.

"Hmm. Well, we could do that, but don't you think Miss Lakely should be doing that? I feel it's our teacher who should be performing her civic duty. We know that she was with the murder victim earlier and on the very same day he was murdered. And, since she obviously knows him, she should identify him to the police," he said.

"Yeah, that's a good point. We need not get involved. I think we should just wait until she comes forward. Unfortunately, she's in Chicago to take care of some of her own personal emergencies," Becky commented.

"You know, that is interesting. Remember how Jack told Miss Lakely he wanted to finish off this job here *and get back home to Chicago*? That could be another clue."

"Yeah, but let's wait and see what develops before we get ourselves into something maybe we shouldn't be involved with right now." Becky picked up her small, leather shoulder bag, stopped by the backyard to thank Mrs. Abbot, and left.

* * *

The rest of the week went by with no further public news reports from the North Haven Police. With each new summer day, Becky and Andy spent more time together. With all they had been through since mid-June, they had developed a special bond sealed with their secrets.

But now, with the unexpected break from their summer school course, they spent the next few days doing normal things that teens do. They went to the beach to swim and to be with their other friends. They also made it to the public golf range to practice hitting balls and improving their swings. There were opportunities to work together on their Logic course project at either one of their homes. And, they managed to do all of these things without bringing up the murder case, even though they waited anxiously to learn if Miss Lakely had contacted the local police.

But when Monday morning finally came and they sat at their desks in Room 205 for the Logic class, their teacher showed no change in her usual personality. She appeared oblivious to the recent and nearby murder.

Becky and Andy waited for Miss Lakely to digress and acknowledge the crime or perhaps the victim. But nothing was forthcoming. Instead, she joked with the students about the summer vacation already going by too quickly and wanted to know how the kids were spending their time away from school. She showed no signs of mourning the death of her friend, Jack.

"Today class, I want to review the topic we discussed earlier on paradoxes. I believe Mr. Pratt gave you the homework assignment. Later, we'll take a look at your examples. Later this week, we're going to begin to learn how to build a 'decision tree.' And that critical topic will take us straight through to the end of this summer course.

"And just as a general introduction, you all should know that decision tree logic is the most common diagnostic tool used in any logic process. I want you all to feel comfortable with it. It is actually a very natural function but now there are 'decision tree software' packages available, where you can plug in the scenario and the hypothesis. After entering other variables into the computer program, the software will guide you through making decisions.

Now, I don't want you to use that, and it's quite pricey anyway. But, I do want you all to develop your own decision tree logic. I'm sure you've all seen it used on TV programs such as 'Cold Case', and that enigmatic medical doctor who often uses it on 'House.' In both shows, the actors draw decision-tree diagrams on white boards to help them visually diagnose or solve difficult mysteries."

Miss Lakely smiled again then asked the class if they had any questions about the plans for the rest of the course. The kids were quiet but with renewed anticipation.

"But before we get into all that, let's begin our group discussion first on paradoxes and some personal paradoxical events."

The students responded enthusiastically, happy to have the young teacher and her vivacious energy back inside the classroom. The class time once again went by too quickly with Miss Lakely in charge. Soon the students were leaving the school to enjoy the remainder of another pleasant summer day.

As Andy walked down the main corridor and headed for the outside door, he felt a hand grab his arm tightly. It held him back from advancing any further. He turned to face his friend's quizzical face.

"Hey, what's this all about, Becky?"

"Don't you think you're going in the wrong direction? The office is down the hall this way, where you and I are going to report for work."

"Oh, hell! Are you sure you want to do this? I mean, what are we really going to find out about what Amber experienced? She worked in the office way back in April. We are already in the month of July for God's sake! We aren't going to learn anything about her job there filing forms and mailing out envelopes."

Becky ignored his remark. She kept hold of his arm and marched him along the empty hallway. The two of them turned into the central administrative office.

The middle-aged secretary, Mrs. Savoyski, greeted the two of them warmly and became enthusiastic when Becky explained why they were there. It was obvious the middle-aged woman was excited to have some student help for the summer. She showed them around and pointed out where files were located. The older woman then explained some of the clerical tasks that would be assigned to each of them. When the orientation was done, Andy and Becky told the older woman they'd work for one to two hours each day beginning the next morning after class. They all felt comfortable with the routines and the computer work required of them.

After they left the school building they once again avoided the Peck's Pond shortcut and chose to walk along Washington Avenue.

"If she didn't inform the police who the murder victim was, we have a freakin' problem, Becky. I mean, damn, why didn't she just tell the cops she and Jack were friends or whatever?"

"I know. I've been thinking about that. I was disappointed she never mentioned anything to the class this morning. She never brought the...the incident up. But we have to give her the benefit of the doubt. She told us she just got back in town last night. Hey, for all we know, maybe she's down at the police station right now. And the cops might want to keep it under wraps for a while until they learn more about ol' Jack. But if she didn't and we go forward and tell the police, we'll be ratting on our own teacher."

"I hope she does that too. Or maybe we're gonna have to confront her on our own. We can come right out and ask her if she did go to the cops. And if she didn't go to the cops, maybe she'll tell us why...unless..."

"Unless what, Andy?"

"Unless...unless Miss Lakely is the one...the one who murdered Jack and dumped him in the pond."

Becky stared without saying a word. She sidestepped the thought with another question.

"Do you think she still does any work in that old underground office, Andy?"

"I'm not sure. We still don't know what the heck kind of work she was doing down there. "

"Well, maybe that's where we start! If we're going to analyze this whole thing we need to first have a theory or a *hypothesis* just like she told us in class this morning. If she was doing something illegal, we must determine that first."

Andy appreciated his friend's professorial demeanor. He cheerfully thought how he could identify more with words like *hypothesis* than a *nickel-defense* on a football field. It was one of the many things the teens shared in common.

"That makes sense...but how do we do that?" Andy asked.

"We've got to get back into that underground office to look for any evidence as to what was really going on down there. Once we can get inside, we can look for clues that will tell us more about this weird mystery and perhaps what our teacher was doing with Jack down there."

Andy's face suddenly drained of all color. He looked as if he would become sick.

"Oh, damn, Becky! I gotta tell you, that old, dirty factory really gives me the creeps. The darkness, those moldy, dirty tunnels crawling with all sorts of creatures and even the freakin' bats all scare the crap out of me. I...I personally never planned to return there ever again after we got my camcorder and our bikes."

Becky smiled, once again appreciating her friend's honesty and candor. "Maybe we don't have to crawl down that hatchway and walk along those tunnels."

"Huh? But how are we going to get into the underground office?"

"Well, we know Miss Lakely didn't use the same hatchway that we did to get inside nor did she use it to get out of there. Remember, we saw how she came in through that far door entrance to the office? And right after she left, she was soon in her car and driving out by the time we were just climbing up the steel ladder to get our butts the hell out of there."

"Yeah, that's true. But how are we going to find out how she got in there? We know she couldn't use the existing entrances. They're all secured with heavy padlocks," said Andy.

"I don't know. I haven't figured that out yet."

Andy's eyes suddenly widened and his face lit up. "Hey, I got it! What if we use Google Earth and look at a bird's eye view of all those old factory buildings on Hook Island? We might learn how she got into the office. There may be another entrance we haven't discovered yet."

Becky once again stared at him. She knew he wasn't a whirlwind jock. And at times he was short on courage. But she was still very much attracted to his honest personality and creative mind.

"Hey, let's go to my house, Andy, and get working on this!"

* * *

Later, inside Becky's neat and orderly bedroom, the two sat once again on her bed, using her laptop computer. Becky selected the desktop icon to launch Google Earth. Within minutes they had a bird's-eye view of the abandoned factories on Hook Island. From that perspective they could easily see how the shape of the island resembled a large fish hook; hence its name.

"Becky, if I'm right about those subterranean steam-heat tunnels, all of these buildings are interconnected under the ground. You know, just like that tunnel we found leading to the office. So, if we look at the pattern of structures, we can find another path to the office doorway Miss Lakely may have used."

The screen images moved around as Becky navigated the cursor with her fingertip.

"There! Right there!" Andy pointed to a structure on the satellite-captured image in the middle of the computer screen.

"Yeah, I see it! It looks like that's the remains of an old, brick smoke-stack or chimney that had been demolished. That must have been the power plant building that housed the company's central furnace. If we think of how the steam tunnels interconnect to each building for the heating pipes, we can figure out how Miss Lakely got inside."

"Okay, let's figure it out."

"Well, look, Beck. That dilapidated shack off to the side must also connect to the furnace building and Building C1 in order for the steam heat to reach it. I think that is the link. If we check it out, I know we'll find a way into the office."

"Can I convince you that we should check it out this afternoon?" she asked him.

"Sure, but Becky, do you realize what we just did?"

"Huh, no, what? What did we just do?" she asked, a puzzled expression churning her face.

"We just used deductive reasoning logic. We went from the general to the specific. Our thesis was that all of the buildings were heated through a network of steam tunnels. We then proved it by looking at all of the island buildings from an aerial view on Google Earth. That showed us a networked map of each building relative to the former power plant. There was only one other building between the brick chimney building that we deduced was the main power plant and our target, building CI. Then we further logically deduced that the particular building would have a steam heating tunnel connecting it to building CI where the office was located. And if our logic is correct, we'll discover another entry into the office by way of the underground steam tunnel network."

Becky couldn't hold back from giggling with her friend's dry, analytical observations.

"My God! You...you are such a crazy, nerdy, goof! Do you know that, Andy Abbot?"

Becky continued to laugh then pushed him hard so that he fell backwards on her bed. But after Becky set her laptop down, her tall friend suddenly retaliated.

Andy reached up to grab her arm. His grip pulled her so she fell back on the bed on top of him. Her jet-black hair flew out as she tumbled down. When her body fell on top of him her laughing tempo slowed, finally turning into a soft and sweet smile. She looked down at Andy lying on her bed staring up at her. Her coal-black eyes pierced into his deep-blue eyes. She could read his mind. She knew at this instant he had no more interest in talking about the mysterious murder, Hook Island, or any theoretical logic. His eyes told her he was only thinking about Becky Bing and nothing but Becky Bing.

For a quiet moment, they just lay on the bed, her body on top of his, looking into each other's eyes. They didn't say a word. It was peaceful; it was comforting for both.

Slowly, gently, he pulled her head down closer to his until they could sense each other's breathing and the thumping of young hearts. His fingers gently massaged her hand and caressed her smooth, soft skin.

Then she lowered her head toward his as she closed her eyes. It was a new experience for both of them. Their lips met, gently and sweetly tasting one another.

Andy moved back slowly. But Becky raised her arm, letting it envelope her friend lying on her bed. Her fingers now caressed his still, soft face, gliding across his skin. The gentle touch gave Andy a new, tingling sensation in his body.

Then Becky pulled his head toward her own and kissed him again; this time more forceful. She now pressed her lips hard against his, wanting him to know how she felt. Andy responded by bringing his arm around Becky, pulling her body closer into his own.

Just as they parted, catching their breath, a voice shouted out from somewhere downstairs jerking them out of the blissful moment.

"Hey, Andy, I just wanted to know if you'd like to join us here for lunch," Becky's mom asked.

The two immediately started giggling, their bodies still pressed together on top of the bed.

"Ah...no, Mrs. Bing," Andy shouted back. "I have to be going home. I'm supposed to cut my neighbor's lawn later this afternoon. But, thank you."

Becky sat up and pulled Andy up by the arm. "Say, that was a good comeback, Mr. Abbot!"

"Hey, I wasn't lying. I promised to cut Mr. Honeywell's lawn while he and his wife are vacationing in Italy."

Becky reacted with a faux pout on her face.

"Oh, so now I'm playing second fiddle to a lawn mower, eh?"

They chuckled and kissed lightly once more before heading downstairs. But they both knew that today they had crossed a fragile line. They had been classmates, fellow band members, and good friends, but now that all changed with the kiss. They could add something else to the list of common interests. Now they were romantically linked and entered into their first young adult relationship. They were now boyfriend and girlfriend.

Their faces beamed bright with happiness as Becky walked Andy to the front door. They were now going to enjoy being with one another more than ever before on a new, more personal level.

CHAPTER TWELVE

The next day was heating up once again as the two pedaled over the wooden bridge crossing over Hook River.

After hiding their bikes in the alley they headed directly toward the crumbled brick structure seen on Google Earth. From there they turned, assuming an underground steam tunnel, and spotted another entranceway to the factory complex.

They walked speedily toward the old, faded green painted door. They found it closed tight, but surprisingly, it was unlocked. After panning around for signs of any life, they opened the weathered exterior door, making a creaking noise. They quietly stepped down a set of decayed, wooden stairs that brought them below the ground level. There were another two doors ahead of them. One, straight ahead, was closed but the one to their right was wide open. Andy grabbed Becky's hand tightly and led the way into what appeared to be an old, utility workshop.

In the afternoon shadows they saw antiquated work benches with old, rusted, steel vices attached to them. A few centipedes, spiders, and other crawling insects were adhering to the bumpy cement walls. Empty cabinets looked as if they had once contained tools and hardware supplies. The two of them quickly turned and left the room, knowing it led them nowhere.

Andy opened the other door and immediately stepped inside the underground office. He turned on the light switch and walked around the dusty and grimy room. It was the same office in which they had witnessed Miss Lakely and her friend, the now deceased, Jack, have their intense meeting.

"Look, there's the tunnel door and window leading to building C1 right over there," Andy said, pointing to the opposite side of the abandoned, dingy room.

"Hey, check it out, Andy. There's another steel door at the back of this office. We couldn't see that from the angle from where we spying. I wonder where that leads."

They walked over to the heavy steel door that had no windows. Andy pulled on it forcefully but found it was locked. There was a key lock beneath the rusted steel handle.

Thinking quickly, Becky turned and stepped over to the old metal desk where Miss Lakely sat during their recent spying session. She pulled open the center drawer. Inside was a sparse supply of pencils, pens, and paper clips. But in one of the drawer compartments there was a chrome key ring with a single key on it.

"Hey, Andy, catch!"

She tossed the key ring in the air to Andy.

The key easily fit into the door lock. The steel door opened to nothing but darkness. Nervous, Andy reached around the corner. He fingered a light switch and flipped it on.

But he didn't move. He just stood frozen in place at the door's threshold. Finally he made a sound.

"Oh, my God! I don't freakin' believe it!"

"What...what is it, Andy?" Becky asked, still standing behind the desk.

"This is quite a surprise and it doesn't belong to Hook Textiles," he shouted a little louder.

Becky rushed over to where Andy was standing. She stood behind him then peeked around his tall frame into the lighted room. She immediately understood his shock.

The room looked nothing like the rest of the old, defunct, factory structure. It was clean and appeared to be in an antiseptic condition. There were no dirty, damp walls with creepy insects scurrying about. The room wasn't dark, but had a modern, organized appearance. The long room had been remodeled recently with bright white painted walls and immaculate tiled flooring. There were several overhead florescent light fixture attached to the suspended tile ceiling. The updated illumination brightened the small room in dramatic contrast to the rest of the building.

But it wasn't just another room. It had been fitted up into a pristine laboratory. In the center of the lab were two stainless steel workbenches set up side by side. A variety of glass beakers, an electronic scale, and large compound mixers rested on the shiny, clean shelves lining the room. There were also several glass containers filled with different powders and chemical substances. As they took a mental inventory, they spotted Pyrex test-tubes in holders standing up in holders on top of shiny steel counters.

"My God, it's a freakin' chemical laboratory, Andy."

"I wonder what the hell they make here," he asked, dumbfounded at the discovery.

Becky looked around and spotted some unmarked, cardboard shipping cartons stacked in a corner of the lab.

She opened a flap of one of the cartons. With one hand, she lifted out one of many plastic sandwich zip-lock bags. The remaining bags all appeared to be the same size and weight. Inside of each transparent bag were small, white pills. They looked similar to aspirin tablets. She guessed there were about fifty pills in each small bag.

"Well, you can bet these are not vitamins," Becky said, before dropping the plastic bag back into the carton.

The teens stepped gingerly around the laboratory, impressed with the professional setup and its stark cleanliness. They walked in silence taking in every aspect of the hidden operation.

Suddenly, a noise startled them, breaking the silence of the lab. It came from outside of the building. The unexpected interruption sounded like a car door slamming shut.

In a panic, they quickly turned off the lab lights and closed the heavy steel door which locked automatically. Andy slapped off the office wall switch bringing blackness to the room. When they found themselves bumping into desks and each other in the dark, damp office, Becky grabbed his arm and yanked him behind her.

"Come, we gotta hurry!" Becky whispered.

She swiftly led him toward the other grimy, windowed door leading to the steam tunnel. It was where they had first discovered the office. She opened it, and they both slipped out of the office and into the musty, steam tunnel.

Just as they shut the door, the office light switch clicked on once again. But the teens were too nervous to pop up to see who had just entered. They hoped whoever it was didn't discover anything out of place.

They next heard the sound of a desk chair rolling on the cement floor followed by a metal desk drawer opening. The subsequent sound was the distinct noise of a hand groping and searching inside that drawer.

Becky instantly knew what was happening. She grimaced in the damp, smelly darkness before she reached out for Andy's hand. The stolen key ring with the lab key was still clutched inside of his sweaty fist.

A brief silence hung in the musty air.

Still squatting anxiously by the door, they heard a man's voice speaking in a low, muffled tone, making it difficult to hear what he was saying. But with ears pressed to the door, they could make out the gist of the phone conversation.

"Hey, boss, when you get this message, call me. It's ah…now three-thirty. The lab keys aren't in the drawer like they're supposed to be. So…right now, I can't get into the lab and pick up the product. Call me after you get this message. I'm leaving here for now and will await your instructions. If you have the key, I can come back here later."

They next heard the office chair rolling and saw that the office lights were turned off. The sound of the other office door slamming shut ended the unexpected visit.

Becky let out a deep, audible sigh.

"Okay, let's get the hell out of here, now!" Andy whispered, not hiding his nervousness. "This is getting too freakin' creepy for me. We shouldn't be here, Becky. I…I really want to get out of here and get back home."

"No, no, wait a minute, shh…"

The sound of a whirring car ignition was soon followed by the noise of rubber tires moving along the asphalt lot outside.

Becky again grabbed Andy's hand. She could feel the nervous vibration but it was difficult to determine if the shaking came from his hand, hers, or both. She pulled the key ring out of his cramped palm.

With her free hand she turned the doorknob, pushed the door open, and ran back into the office. Still dragging Andy behind her, she felt around in the darkness for the metal desk drawer. After finding it, she pulled it open and returned the key inside.

They ran out of the darkened office and were soon out of the building breathing in the fresh, salty air. Within minutes the two were pedaling quickly back toward Beechwood Knoll.

After reaching Beechwood Knoll they pulled their bikes up in front of Smitty's Diner. Sitting inside a booth, they sipped iced lemonade through straws. They spoke in a whisper.

"Becky, I got to tell you. I really, really don't like any of this crap that's happening. This is all way over my head and I'm getting really scared. We're into some weird shit that we shouldn't be, Becky, and I want out!"

"I know, I know," she said with a nod, after sucking the chilled liquid up through her plastic straw. Her eyes glazed over for a moment as she thought. It was a few minutes before she spoke again.

"It's just that nothing makes sense to me, Andy. And now this guy, who we didn't see, came into the drug lab. You know, it's kinda weird, but I think I've heard his voice before. But I can't place the voice with a face right now. Did that voice sound familiar to you?"

"Ah, well, I don't know. I'm not sure. It was difficult eavesdropping through the door. And the tone was very low. But in a way, it did sound a little familiar, but I can't seem to place it, either. It's like something you think you know you see, but you're not sure. Then it turns out to be something entirely different."

"Yeah, I know what you mean. We don't want to jump to any conclusions. It's just like what Miss Lakely wrote on the white board. Do you remember? Things are not always what they seem to be."

Andy pondered the coincidence. "Yeah, I remember her writing that sentence the other day. It didn't make a lot of sense at first, you know, like some deep philosophical stuff."

They each sipped the iced lemonade.

"Hey, that reminds me of the tiny light we spotted in the video that night of the New Age jam session. We still don't know what it was, yet we know something was moving around in the darkness of the factory. And I talked to my dad on the phone last night. I asked him about his computer's image-enhancing software. He told me I could use it anytime and told me how to get into the program. So, did you download any freeze frames of that tiny light moving around?"

"Ah…no, but I don't think you're listening to me, Becky. We need to back away from all of this crap. I mean, what the hell are we doing snooping around like secret spies, or private investigators, for God's sake? This is no game, you know. The freakin' stakes are too high. That poor guy, Jack whoever, already got shot to death. I don't want you or me to be the next victim in this twisted bullshit."

Becky understood. She reached across the table and gently took his hand into hers.

"You're right, Andy. But…but let's just give it a rest for a day or so. We need to get away from it. Besides, the North Haven Police are going to have another press conference soon. Let's see what they come up with before we consider going to them."

"Just give it a rest? What do you think we should do?"

"I think tomorrow we should forget about all of this and go somewhere…you know, somewhere for our first date."

Andy smiled. It was his first grin in hours.

"I agree," he replied, now gently squeezing her hand still entwined with his. "But where would you like to go on our first date?"

"Oh, I don't know…how about…."

Just then Becky's cell phone rang. She reached down and pulled it out of her shorts side pocket. Her face look surprised after she read the caller ID.

"Oh, hello Amber! I'm…I'm just fine. How are you?"

Andy's eyebrows arched, hearing the name. He quietly drained his lemonade while listening.

Becky looked at him while she spoke into the cell.

"Oh, that's not a problem, Amber. Don't worry about it. I didn't think anything of it. Huh? Oh yeah. I'd love that. Sure, I think it would be great fun. Tomorrow afternoon? Oh, but…I did have a date planned with Andy, but I can….”

Another pause.

“Really? No, no, I’m sure he’d love to come along. Oh, yeah, I know he will.”

Pause.

“Thanks, sure. Let’s meet at the corner of Bridge Street. One o’clock? That’ll be fine. See you then.”

Becky’s eyes widened as she flipped her cell closed.

“Well, you heard almost everything. Amber got my cell number from one of my friends. She called to tell me she felt bad. She was sorry about how she acted the other day. You know, when she stormed away from us. With her apology to me and to you, she wants to make it up. So she offered to take us to the Yale Golf Course tomorrow for eighteen holes.”

“No kidding! Yale’s course is supposed to be awesome!”

“Yeah, and she also has her mother’s car for all day tomorrow. She’ll pick us up at one o’clock.”

“So our first date will be playing golf!” Andy grinned.

They both giggled with a naturally childish reaction to the surprise invitation and the anticipation to play golf together.

Once again, it was good for them to laugh and to be the positive young kids they still were. The unexpected lightness took them away from the scary events they had experienced.

CHAPTER THIRTEEN

At precisely one o'clock the next afternoon, Amber drove up to the corner of Bridge Street. She was behind the wheel of an older model Ford Explorer, SUV.

Andy opened the rear hatch door and laid their golf bags gently on top of Amber's already stored inside. Becky jumped into the passenger seat and pulled on her seat belt. Andy slipped into the rear seat.

The three of them chatted as the SUV meandered around the streets headed toward the city of New Haven. Most of their conversation covered school courses they were all taking in the fall. Amber told them how she was anxious to finish her senior year and get into college and away from North Haven.

"I've applied to Cornell, Colgate, and Ithaca colleges and will be hearing back from them real soon."

"Hey! It sounds like you really want to live in upstate New York," Becky commented.

"I do! My aunt, uncle, and cousins live up there and we all get along so well. I love it up there in the autumn but especially during the winter with all the ski slopes."

Becky and Andy noticed a different person in Amber today. She seemed much more relaxed and more congenial. Her inner personality now paralleled her outer beauty.

After renting pull-carts from the Pro Shop, the three of them walked down a hill and headed toward the elevated tee box for the first hole. Since it was summer and later in the day, the university's course was not busy.

The eighteen-hole round of golf was good for all three of them. Amber shot a low score of 76. Becky's score card recorded an 88. Andy was pleased just "breaking 100" with his 99. When they finished their round, after nearly five hours out on the picturesque course, the three teens looked forward to sitting down for a cold drink back inside of the clubhouse. They sat in a quiet corner of the small restaurant. There were only a few other adults sitting at the bar a distance away with all eyes riveted onto the bar's TV screen. From where they were sitting they could recognize the legendary green wall of Fenway Park. The Boston Red Sox were hosting a game with the New York Yankees.

"So, are you enjoying our summer Logic course?" Becky asked Amber.

"Oh, hell yeah! I really like Miss Lakely. She is just too cool. I wish she had been at North Haven during my junior year. She…she is so open with us! And she's really not a phony. That's what I like about her. What you see is what you get!"

"Ha! Oh, I wouldn't be so sure about…" Andy began.

Becky's swift kick to Andy's shin stopped him mid-sentence.

"Amber, we only got a few weeks left of summer school. And I hate to bring up a sore subject with you, but Andy and I both start working in the school office tomorrow."

The pink hue in Amber's face suddenly drained. The vibrant sunshine vanished from her sparkling eyes.

"Are you really going to work in that dreadful office?"

"Yeah, we are. And we were, ah…kinda concerned about what you told us. I mean, it just made no sense to us. But we also know you had worked there during the April vacation. Isn't that right?"

Amber seemed surprised and she took a long swig of her diet soda. Then she slowly lowered her head facing only the clubhouse table. There was no response to Becky's question. The attractive blonde appeared to be going through a private moment.

Andy squirmed around anxiously in his chair. He was uncomfortable watching a stressful moment tighten its grip around the young woman.

She finally raised her head and looked at Becky and then Andy. Her eyes had now become watery with tears.

"Look, I realize I don't know you two, or at least, know you very well. But somehow I want to trust you. I'm...I'm going to tell you things I've never told anyone before. And, I need you to promise, and I mean really, really promise, not to repeat any of what I tell you. I also think it might help me, in a way, if I tell... someone."

Becky sensed the other girl's intense emotional conflict. She leaned into the table to get closer and spoke in a soft, sincere voice.

"We won't tell a soul, we promise, Amber."

Amber hesitated as a spontaneous roar sounded from the bar area. The TV cameras focused on a Red Sox player rounding the bases with an extra innings homerun. The Sox had won this game against the traditional rival team.

The older patrons now paid their bar bills, swiveled off of the stools, and left the club house restaurant. The teens were now the only customers in the facility.

Amber continued. "Like you, I learned the school office needed help during April vacation. And, of course, I needed the money. So, I applied for the job and Mrs. Savoyski hired me. The plan was for me to work each day from eight in the morning until three in the afternoon during that vacation week. The first couple of days went well and I really enjoyed the work. Mrs. Savoyski gave me simple assignments, but it helped her out a lot and gave her a little break. I liked the work and the time seemed to go by quickly."

Amber paused, and Becky sensed the girl's struggle and need for composure. She interrupted to give her more time.

"And, that's what I'd expect too, Amber. Not much pressure, casual work, but still helping out," she commented. "Sounds just like what Andy and I are expecting."

"Yeah, but what I didn't know was that Mrs. Savoyski was only working the first three days during that vacation week. She had plans to take Thursday and Friday off. So late on that Wednesday, she told me that Mr. Pratt would be the only one to come in on Thursday and Friday and he'd give me my daily assignments. Mrs. S told me he might have some special projects that required some computer work, and that I'd be a big help since he was not especially good using the computer. I remember how she confided in me that our principal was a 'needy' man, especially since his wife had passed away a few years back."

"Well," Andy interjected. "That sure as hell doesn't surprise me. I mean, I can believe the 'old silver fox' is far from being a computer wizard!"

The remark went without any acknowledgment.

"So how was it working in the office for those last two days?" Becky probed.

Amber took in a deep breath and exhaled.

"Well, Thursday was okay. In fact, it was fine. But Mr. Pratt did spend a lot of time talking to me. I remember he even bought me my favorite cold drink, a Diet Coke, after seeing me have one the previous day. Then he began asking me some personal stuff about my college plans, boyfriends and girlfriends, movies I liked, and all that shit. But it was fine. I thought he was just trying to be personable and get to know me a little better. But it was on that afternoon that I had to tell him I might be a little late coming in on Friday morning. I told him I had to drive my folks to the New Haven train station. They were going to New Jersey for a family funeral and wouldn't be back until Sunday. He jokingly asked if I was going to have a 'party weekend' with my parents being away.

"I told him I wasn't the partying type and had to watch my younger brother. I had also made plans for my best friend, Sandy, to come stay with me while my parents were away." Amber paused for a moment. "Sandy and I were both looking forward to it!"

"So, I don't get it. I mean it sounded like you had a good week," Andy said.

"Well, the week wasn't over and the problem wasn't in the office."

"Huh?"

Amber took another nervous swig of her soda and continued.

"I came into the empty office about ten o'clock on that Friday morning. With nobody around, I just straightened up the files and papers for Mrs. Savoyski for when she returned on Monday."

"And so, where was Mr. Pratt?" Andy asked.

"He came in a little later. I noticed that he seemed shook up about something. I figured it was something personal and let it go. Besides, I really didn't want to know. But then he approached me and asked for a big favor. He told me his desktop computer had just come up with some weird technical problem. The computer was at his vacation cottage up on Bantam Lake. That's where he had been the previous night. I only knew Bantam was up in northern Connecticut almost an hour's drive from here."

"Yeah, I've been up to Bantam Lake. It's really nice up there," Andy added.

Becky and Amber stared blankly at him.

"Anyway, Mr. Pratt asked if I could take a drive up there with him to try to fix the desktop computer problem. He told me we'd be back at the school by early afternoon. He also told me I could go home then and he'd still pay me for a full eight hours. How...how could I say no? After all, he's my principal and he now needed my help."

"That makes sense! I probably would have done the same thing," Andy added. Becky stared at Andy across the small restaurant table, a piercing look of unspoken admonition.

"So what happened? Did...did you make the trip up there with him?" Becky asked.

"So, I got into his car with him and he drove us up to Bantam Lake. It was nearly noon by the time we got there. He had a large, log cabin styled house that was built recently. It was very nice but located in a desolate part of the Bantam woods. I remember how the dirt roads were all muddy after the recent April rains.

"When we got inside, he showed me around and told me where the bathroom was. I went there while he answered his cell phone."

Andy and Becky could picture the scene of this beautiful, innocent young lady out in the densely wooded part of Connecticut with an older man she hardly knew. They now sensed her extreme nervousness as she unfolded her story. More pauses and gaps in her sentences now occurred as though she was carefully planning her words.

Becky waited for a moment before speaking.

"Amber, are you all right?"

The beautiful girl nodded her head in silence as tears rolled down her cheeks.

"I...I came out of the bathroom. Mr. Pratt was on the living room sofa. An HP desktop computer was set up on a small table in front of him. He told me about the technical problems. I figured I could just run some utility programs like the disk organizer, along with defragmenter and spyware protection programs to see if that's what caused his problems."

"So...did you try those software tools?" Andy asked.

"No. I was about to begin working, but Mr. Pratt had already poured a cold drink for me and he seemed only to want to talk. It was another Diet Coke already poured into a tall glass with ice cubes in it. He cracked opened another can and poured it in a glass of ice for himself. So we chatted for a while. He told me how he comes up to his cabin to unwind often. He pointed out through the screened windows the beauty of the land, the deer, and other small animals that come onto his property and all that crap. I wanted to get by the small talk so I turned to the desktop computer and booted it up."

Amber suddenly stopped talking. A long pause hung in the clubhouse air.

"Amber, what happened next? Did you make any progress debugging his computer?" Andy asked, focusing now on the technical sidebar rather than the point of her personal story. .

The young girl dropped her head down into her palms.

"I wish I could answer that. But the truth is…I don't remember anything that happened. And that's the problem, or at least the beginning of the problem."

"You don't remember? Why not?" Andy asked.

"I'm telling you, the last thing I remember was sitting next to Mr. Pratt on that sofa. I had logged onto his computer and was sipping my soda. After that, my mind...or my memory is a blank."

"Oh, my God! Was there something in your soda? Did Pratt put something into your drink?" Becky asked with sharp anger in her voice.

With her head still buried in her hands, Amber nodded.

"Yes, yes I think so. That's the only thing I can think happened. I…I just don't know. The last clear thing I can recall is having that glass of soda. It wasn't in a can or a bottle. He already had poured it in a tall glass for me. Then after taking a few sips everything becomes so confusing… and…and lost."

"But Amber, do you remember anything? Anything at all?"

"Oh…believe me. I've been through this a thousand times. I get these mental images, blurry images of some weird sights and sounds, but nothing I can piece together."

A tense quiet suddenly filled the emptied golf course restaurant. Amber kept her head down, now with a tissue to her face.

Becky was uncomfortable and looked over to Andy sitting opposite her, who looked just as uncomfortable with the story. But there had to be more to this. An awkward tension now enveloped the three of them. It was the yet unspoken climax that made Andy squirm once again with anxiety. He had to break the silence.

"Amber, was there…was there any more after that? I mean, when did you regain your clear mind?"

She looked up at the two new friends. Her eyes were now a blurred and watery red color. It was apparent she was trying to garner enough courage to continue.

Stunned with the story, Andy and Becky felt compassion swelling within them, the likes of which they had never felt before in their young lives.

Amber explained again this was the first time she had told anyone what had happened to her. She had never found the courage to tell her closest friends or her parents. But for some strange reason, today she opened up to Becky Bing and Andy Abbot after a pleasurable round of golf.

"I can't tell you anything else that happened. The next thing I can remember was waking up inside his cabin bedroom. I…I had no idea where I was. The room was so…so foreign to me. I was on top of the bed covers, but still fully clothed.

"I slowly got up from the bed and stepped out of the bedroom. There was some dizziness and my stomach didn't feel so good. I felt ready to vomit. As I walked into the living room, Mr. Pratt was still on the sofa now working on his desktop computer. Then everything came back to me like a re-run of a video. I remembered why I had come up to this remote cabin. But, I couldn't remember anything beyond sitting on the couch and drinking the Diet Coke."

"What did our...our principal say to you when you came out of the bedroom?"

"He asked me how I felt. He then told me I had suddenly fainted on his sofa. According to Pratt, he helped me lay down on top of the guest bed. Supposedly, I fell into a deep sleep. He told me he thought I was coming down with the flu or something.

"'I think you were a little run down, Amber,' he told me. 'You became suddenly drowsy after looking at my computer and told me you needed to lie down.' Then he told me more bullshit. He thought a little nap would make me feel better. I was still feeling so sick. I... I just believed what he had told me. I had no reason to think otherwise."

"Then what happened?" Andy asked.

"We left the cottage. He drove me back to the high school where I had parked my mother's car. On the drive home, I checked my cell and answered a text. It was from my friend, Sandy. She was already at my house and was ready for the 'sleepover'. She had been wondering why the hell I wasn't there. It wasn't until then that I realized how late it was in the day. I had been sleeping on that bed for well over three hours!"

"So, do you think you really had been sick, and kinda, you know, passed out at Mr. Pratt's cabin?" Becky asked.

"No, I wasn't sick at all before...before I got to that cabin. I had been feeling fine." Tears quickly welled up in Amber's blurred blue eyes. Her face took on a strange contortion and her chin trembled uncontrollably. And then she blurted out the shocking announcement, nearly loud enough for the female bartender to hear.

"Don't you understand? I was raped!" Tears raced down her face as she now sobbed loudly.

Becky reached out and took Amber's hand into her own. The club's bartender rushed over to check on the trio at the table.

"Is everything all right over here?" the middle-aged woman asked. They all nodded.

"Ah…we're fine thanks," Becky answered.

The woman returned to her post behind the bar.

Andy pulled some napkins from the holder in the middle of the table and handed them to the emotionally-wrought girl. She put her head down and took some deep, loud breaths. After dabbing her eyes with the paper napkins, she lifted up her head.

"I'm sorry. I'm so sorry to lay all of this shit on the two of you. It took a while to realize I had been raped. I really didn't plan on telling anyone about what happened. I couldn't tell my parents, the police, or anyone else. I…I had been completely out of it. But the physical signs were there. And since I don't remember anything, I couldn't tell anyone what really happened."

"Do you remember Mr. Pratt bringing you into the bedroom?" Becky asked.

"No. I…I don't have any memory of Mr. Pratt after drinking from that glass of soda. But…the strangest thing is that now I keep on having weird dream fragments or flashbacks that pop into my mind. They're like nightmares that come while I'm awake during the day. They pop into my mind without any warning. Some are visions but others are things I hear; unusual sounds. It's like some creepy horror movie that plays in my head."

"Really? Like what? What's in that movie?" Becky asked.

"In these…these images or whatever the hell they are, I see a strange man looking down at me. This guy is scary. He keeps smiling at me and drooling. I'm telling you this dude is really fucking creepy. And in my dreams or whatever they are, the guy stares at me and is always laughing loudly while looking down on me. I…I think this guy, whoever he is, was the freak who…who raped me."

"But you never saw this creepy guy before, or since that day in the cabin?" Andy asked.

"No, I mean this weirdo is a face anybody would have remembered. I can't forget it even now."

"Amber you just used the word "dreams." Do you think…?"

"No, no the images are real! I'm telling you. I have them all the time when I'm alone, sometimes in the classroom or when I'm alone in my house, or just walking on the beach. They often come back during the night. They're nightmares and often wake me up with me screaming in a sweaty fit."

Andy now understood why Amber was the quietest student in the AP Logic class. She was keeping a dark secret.

Amber glanced up at the clock on the wall. She took a moment, wiping her face with more of the tabletop napkins. After a deep breath and exhaling out loudly she regained some of her composure.

"Hey, we'd better get going. I need to get my mother's car back to her. She's actually going out with my dad tonight to look at a new car. If things work out, she's going to give me her Explorer to drive during senior year."

Andy picked up their paper cups and walked them across the restaurant floor, dumping them in the trash receptacle. As he walked away he could still hear Becky's next question, despite her whispering tone.

"Amber, do you know for sure? I mean, are you convinced you were raped?"

Amber likewise responded in a very low whisper that Andy couldn't hear. Nor did he want to. He knew it was a private discussion and purposely stalled away from earshot of the table conversation. He waited until they were done speaking then joined them to walk outside to the Ford SUV.

"So, again I trust you two will keep this quiet, and I appreciate you listening to me," she said as she started the engine.

"Amber, we're here for you. Don't worry about us keeping this a secret."

The ride back to Beechwood Knoll was quiet with intermittent and awkward attempts at small talk. After Amber pulled up to Andy's house to drop him and his golf bag off at the curbside, he walked up to the driver's side of the vehicle. He leaned in the window to thank Amber and to ask her one more question.

"Amber, you mentioned you had flashbacks of some 'unusual sounds.' Can I ask you what those sounds were?"

Amber quietly thought before responding. She looked blankly through the windshield in front of her then turned to face Andy again.

"Oh, it's going to sound weird, but this one sound keeps coming back again and again. I believe it was something I heard that may have woken me up in that cabin bedroom. It was a motor, but not a car motor, or a lawn mower or anything like that. It was…it was just like the loud sound of a motorcycle starting up."

Andy peered over to Becky still belted into the passenger seat.

"Oh, okay. Thanks again, Amber!" Andy swung his golf bag over his shoulder and marched straight into the garage attached to his family's house. He turned briefly to look back before the car pulled away. He stared inside the front window, not at Amber, but at Becky.

Their eyes connected one last time as the car drove off.

CHAPTER FOURTEEN

Andy and Becky were deeply overwhelmed after listening to Amber's story. Her divulging that she had been raped struck them with a myriad of emotions. They were stunned that a new acquaintance would share such intimate privacy, but once over this hurdle, anger and compassion followed.

The unscheduled event served to divert their nagging obsession with the Peck's Pond murder, Hook Island, and their mysterious teacher, Amanda Lakely.

They had just learned that one of their classmates had been a victim of a heinous sexual assault. But she was not only a victim; she also had no recourse to identify and prosecute her attacker because of the bizarre circumstances. Both Becky and Andy understood if she had gone to the police or to a hospital, she couldn't provide authorities with any information since she was under the influence of drugs. They knew the police would never believe her unsubstantiated story and further, she wouldn't put her family through such a public and shocking ordeal.

Later that night Andy tossed and turned in his bed finding it difficult to fall asleep. He didn't realize it, but the recent events were transitioning him from an adolescent into a man. He remembered his grandfather had once told him that 'coming of age' happens in many ways. But on this night he wasn't thinking of his granddad. His mind was focused on the helpless victim, Amber Woods.

Now he clearly understood why she had suddenly "morphed" from the most popular girl in her class into an introverted recluse. But he could never tell Tyler Farnham about his discovery. Only he and Becky now knew the personal violation she had experienced. And it would stay that way.

Likewise, Becky couldn't fall asleep that night. She rolled back and forth under her bed covers. Her mind kept working, trying to analyze what had happened to Amber.

Why did Mr. Pratt, "the old Silver Fox," really bring her up to his cabin? And, was there another man who participated in the sexual assault? And if so, who the hell was he? What drug was put into her soft drink that desensitized Amber and gave her the amnesia?

Or was the story actually true? She knew she believed Amber, but the story about their principal was clearly over the top. Was there more to this story that Amber didn't tell her and Andy?

She was pleased that she and Andy had taken the part-time job in the school office. She was convinced that after fingering through the files and folders, they'd learn more of what went on at North Haven High School. And that investigating would involve not only the mysterious Miss Lakely, but now the enigmatic Mr. Pratt.

* * *

The next morning, Andy noticed that his girl, Becky, didn't appear to be her bubbly self. He knew full well enough to leave her alone to her private thoughts and refrained from any early morning mental calisthenics.

As they walked up the circular driveway leading to the high school's main entrance, Miss Lakely surprised them by quietly walking up behind them.

Today, the young teacher wore a salmon-colored top with spaghetti straps. Her pair of beige shorts matched her open-toed sandals. Her shoulder bag was an oversized, natural straw model, opened at the top but clasped with a snap button in the middle.

"Hey, you guys, how are you doing? How's the summer going for you two? I hope you're getting some beach time in!"

"Huh? Oh, yeah, Miss Lakely, we've both been to the beach already a few times. Yeah, the summer's goin' great!" Andy responded, feeling a little uneasy chatting with the mysterious teacher. When the three of them stepped along the tiled corridor leading to Room 205, the head janitor, Mr. Jencks, stopped them.

"Oh, good morning, Miss Lakely!" Mr. Jencks said, with his Swedish accent. "I wanted to see you today to give you a 'heads up'. We're going to strip the wax floors on this wing of the building. So, the Faculty Ladies Room will be off limits. Can you use the girls' lavatory just for today?"

"Oh, sure, Mr. Jencks. Thanks for letting me know," the young teacher replied. She turned to the face the two students as they continued their stroll down the hallway.

"So, besides hanging out at the beach, anything exciting going on with you two?"

Becky looked obliquely at her teacher before answering. *Was there anything exciting going on? What the hell did she mean by that? Does she know something or is she just validating the gossip that now Andy and I are going together?*

"Ah, no, not really. We're just relaxing and playing some golf now and then," Becky replied.

"Oh, that sounds good! I haven't been out on the course in a long time. I've got to get out there soon and see if I can still swing the clubs!"

They entered the classroom and took their seats. Becky looked around as the early morning class began.

But today there were only four students in the Logic class. Amber Woods was absent for the first time.

The session went by quickly as it always did. Miss Lakely continued her knack of keeping her students focused and energized on the subject matter. Her interactive presentation was always lively and she appeared to have fun discussing what could be considered by some as a boring subject. The students always felt like they were integrally part of the learning process inside of her classroom.

After class, Andy and Becky ambled out of the classroom, still feeling the somber effects of Amber's story.

"I'm going to the office to tell Mrs. Savoyski I can't work today. I just can't do it today, Andy. I am just too blown away at what happened to Amber."

"Good! Then let's stop at Dunkin' Donuts for a Coolatta on the way home, Becky. I really need some time to talk with you."

"Of course! But right now I have to use the girls' lav. Wait outside by the flagpole for me. I'll be with you in a few minutes."

Andy headed for the main door, stepping past Mr. Jencks working the power floor stripper.

After telling Mrs. Savoyski that she and Andy had other commitments, Becky walked briskly into the lavatory, choosing a stall farthest from the doorway. Soon after she sat down on the toilet, she heard the stall door next to hers open, close, and lock. She immediately recognized the large, natural straw shoulder bag set on the adjacent stall floor.

Miss Lakely was next to her.

Becky heard rustling coming from inside the stall, but then a cell ring tone astonished her. She looked down and saw Miss Lakely's hand reach down and unsnap the clasp button to her bag. Her hand groped around then pulled out her red cell phone.

The conversation was brief and mumbled. Becky thought Miss Lakely must know having a conversation in the bathroom wasn't wise, especially with the next stall being occupied. The dialogue was simple and unrevealing.

"Yeah, I know. I can be there, don't worry. Yeah, I know things are hot right now, but it'll be over soon."

Before Miss Lakely ended the call and put away her cell, Becky stared down at the opened straw handbag on the floor. She couldn't believe what she saw.

There, lying inside the middle of the shoulder bag was a weapon. It was a black metal handgun with a knurled-grip handle. Then it struck her deep within her being. She sat straight up on the toilet seat. *My favorite teacher is into something no good and it might be murder.*

Miss Lakely returned her cell to her oversized handbag and quickly refastened the clasp. Within minutes she was out of the stall walking toward the row of sinks.

Becky sat quietly while she heard the stream of water run from the faucet. Then the sound of the towel dispenser assured her that Miss Lakely was done and on her way out.

Becky waited a few minutes before leaving her stall to wash and exit the lavatory. She stepped quickly out of the building, relieved that she wasn't followed. She soon spotted Andy waiting for her by the school's flagpole.

But when she approached him, she couldn't hide the emotional vulnerability in her eyes. It was as if suddenly everything from the past few weeks had just pushed her to the brink. It had all become too much.

When she looked up at Andy, she tried hard to turn her lips up into a smile but the facial muscles wouldn't let her do that. Without warning, her chin quivered uncontrollably and tears quickly welled up cresting at her eyelids.

Andy looked into her eyes and in an instant, knew what was happening. Naturally and warmly, he opened his arms wide for her. Becky   immediately   fell   into them. She desperately needed to be hugged. Right now she needed to feel someone else's arms around her petite body. Her head snuggled close into his chest. There was a sudden outburst of a sob as her tears rolled down her face and dampened his polo shirt.

But the heartfelt embrace soon made her feel loved inside, protecting her from all of the recent evil and negativity. For the time being, she felt comforted in the safe and loving harbor of Andy Abbot's arms. For several minutes, the world stood still as two young sweethearts were interlocked in the tall, thin shadow of the school flagpole.

Andy held his girlfriend close to him, thinking how the two of them—innocent and naïve— had been thrust into serious adult drama. But as if that wasn't enough, now they'd learned something much darker—a crime against a young, innocent girl, the victim of a sick and unspeakable crime.

The events had taken its emotional effect on both of them. The close tightness of their bodies gave both the reassurance of life and love despite the surrounding negativity.

When Becky regained some composure, she raised her head and gave Andy a soft, heartfelt kiss on his lips. He returned the kiss before they both turned to leave the school grounds. After quietly walking some distance hand in hand, it was Becky who broke the silence.

"I got something to tell you, Andy, but…but listen. I don't want you to jump to any conclusions."

Andy stopped walking. He turned to face her.

"Does it…does it have to do with me, Becky?"

She smiled at the hint of sudden insecurity in his eyes.

"No, no, it's not about you. It's about Miss Lakely."

With large raindrops now falling down upon them, they increased their pace to a jog until they reached the nearby Dunkin' Donuts shop. Inside they collected their order and sat at the small round table in the farthest corner.

"So, what is it now about our beloved teacher, Miss Lakely?"

There would be no teased drama to what she had to tell him. She just let it out.

"She carries a gun in her handbag. I just saw it while I was inside the bathroom."

Andy's eye opened wide after hearing the revelation. The news caused him to choke on his mouthful of cinnamon-raisin bagel. A quick gulp of his iced coffee helped the situation.

"Huh?"

Becky told him once again what she had just seen.

"Oh my God, Beck! Do you...do you think Miss Lakely shot and killed Jack the biker?"

Becky sipped her drink. "Now, see? I just asked you a minute ago NOT to jump to conclusions. And...and here you are—doing just that!"

"Yeah, but don't you understand! We find out our teacher is working part time in some illegal drug mill. And then her accomplice, or friend or whatever, is found shot to death not far from the school where she teaches. She never comes forward to the police. Now you tell me she's carrying a handgun. Jack was killed with a handgun. Why the hell wouldn't I jump to that conclusion?"

"Why? Because we haven't done any in-depth analysis yet. Don't you remember what we learned? In order to perform an accurate diagnosis, we must not be biased or presumptuous. We must avoid prejudice and be aware of the ever present paradox. And, we should examine each of the facts, test them and see how they're connected or related in some way."

Andy sipped his Coffee Coolatta, impressed with her calm, methodical, academic explanation. He was falling in love with this girl.

"And that's exactly what I wanted to talk to you about today, Beck. After yesterday with what we learned about Amber, and this unsolved murder, the drug factory, and our homeroom slash Logic teacher, I just want to give it all up. I mean, I want to see justice carried out, not only in the murder at Peck's Pond but now even more so in Amber's...Amber's..."

"Rape." Becky finished his sentence.

"My point, Beck, is this: I'm not cut out to do this...this crap. I want to swim, goof around, play golf, play X-box and have fun! I mean, hell, we're doing some heavy adult things we shouldn't be at sixteen. And I really want to let it all go. Let's forget everything and get back to having fun, Becky. You know; just you and me."

Becky only smiled as she looked up into his blue eyes now fired up with emotion. She decided to derail the conversation for a moment.

"You look a little tired today. Did you have trouble getting to sleep last night, like I did?"

Andy went for the diversion, as she knew he would.

"Yeah, I tossed and turned for what seemed hours. Then I finally got out of bed and did some things on the computer."

"Oh? Like what things? Did you play X-box with your friends?"

Andy smiled. "No. I had to do something because I was so worked up, so I took out my camcorder and image-captured those shots taken at the factory. You know, those frames with the tiny, jerky, bright light."

A sharp flash of lightning suddenly lit up the sky followed by a loud crack of thunder rumbling through the building. It rattled the cups sitting on the table. They both looked out through the shop window at the darkening clouds and rain that poured down.

"And what did you do with those images?"

Andy took out a flash drive from his cargo shorts pocket. "They're all on here. I figured we could at least try to find out what the hell that thing was on the recording. Don't get me wrong, I'm still convinced we should back away from this stuff, but at least we might solve our own little mystery of the dancing light at the factory. You know, my unyielding curiosity always prevails."

His joking comment made Becky smile. She took out her cell phone and called home. "Hi, Mom! Can you please come by and pick Andy and me up at Dunkin' Donuts? This storm is going to be around for a while." Pause. "Yeah, we have some homework to do, so he'll be staying for lunch. Thanks, Mom!"

Later that morning, instead of going upstairs into Becky's bedroom, she led him directly into Dr. Bing's study. Inside the room were bookshelves filled with textbooks and various reference files. Most of the thick tomes referred to medicine, and in particular, orthopedic surgical topics.

Andy stepped over to a life-sized mock skeleton hanging in the corner of the study.

"Hey, I remember this model skeleton, Beck. Your dad brought it into our Eighth Grade Career Day. He talked to our class about what it was like to become an Orthopedic Surgeon."

Becky smiled. "Yeah, I remember that day, too. Dad and I later nicknamed the skeleton, *GuGe*. It means 'bones' in Chinese."

"Well, hello there, Mr. Bones! I ah…mean *GuGe*," Andy said while lifting one of the skeletal hands and moving it up and down in a playful handshake.

"Let me know if he says 'hello' back," Becky joked.

"Okay, so here's my computer flash drive with the downloaded image frames," he said, handing the small, encased data drive to his friend. "Load it up and launch your dad's image enhancement program. Let's see if we can find out what the hell that tiny spot of moving light is in the video."

They quietly worked together at the computer images, attempting to zoom in on the tiny light surrounded by total darkness inside of the factory.

While they watched the enhancement software lighten up the darkened areas, they began to see something surface very close to the tiny light.

"Andy, look! That's someone's hand on the screen. I knew it was somebody holding a mini-flashlight in the background! Some guy was standing in the dark shadows during that New Age performance."

"My guess is nobody knew he was there snooping on the performance. Whoever it was standing there was spying on the band! Why else would he stand back in the darkness?" Andy responded. "But, if he didn't want anybody to know he was there why would he hold a mini-flashlight standing in the dark? I'm not so sure he was actually spying on the band!"

"Hmm. You have a good point there," Becky answered, still concentrating on the screen image.

She continued to focus on the shadowy image on the computer screen making adjustments and manipulating the image software. Andy stared at the screen image as the light enhancement further clarified the still photo.

"Hey, Becky, look, look! That's not a flashlight being held in someone's hand. Don't you see? It's a shiny ring. It's...it's a paradox."

Becky slowly turned to stare at him.

"Huh? What the fuuuuh...huh? A paradox?"

"Look! It only appears that it was giving off a light beam like a mini-flashlight. But it wasn't giving light. The ring was receiving light. It was a reflection from the lit up stage area lighting, where the band was playing. And the ring's gemstone reflected that light source. And take a look at that freakin' puppy! It appears to be a huge diamond, but it must be zircon or something like that. It's really too huge."

Becky once again fine tuned the image software.

"Yeah, but look! Look at the finger wearing the huge reflecting ring. We can see it now. It's on the pinky finger. And it's a male's pinky finger 'cause it's too big to be a woman's."

The two of them turned and looked at each other. Their mouths hung open. Silence now filled Dr. Bing's office while they stared at the man's large reflective pinky ring.

"Beck, navigate further up on the person's body with the navigator button. Let's see if we can make out the face of the guy with that pinky ring."

Becky tried to enlarge the image but the dark, opaque shadows prevented any improvement on the lumen intensity and pixel resolution. But there was, however, another shining item located a little higher up from the ring. It also appeared to reflect the lighting from the makeshift stage.

"What do you think is reflecting those stage lights higher up on the guy's body?" Andy asked.

"I'd say it looks a lot like a gold chain. Yeah, yeah. There's certainly a thick, gold chain around that guy's neck," Becky said.

They continued trying to enhance the shadowy figure but with no improved success. The mystery person's face was well-hidden in the backdrop of the darkened factory steam tunnel.

"Okay. So, we found someone hiding in the darkness with an enormous ring on the pinky finger. The dude also has a gold chain strung around his neck. Now, who do we know who might wear both of those unusual items?" Andy's question was a rhetorical one but also a leading one for Becky.

"Well, there's only one such dude I know of who has those things. That would be our former homeroom teacher, Mr. Barry Jones."

"You got it," Andy said. "Mr. Jones is the only one I know who would have such jewelry."

CHAPTER FIFTEEN

Shortly after noontime, Mrs. Bing called out to the two teens still sitting in the first floor study.
"Lunch is ready, kids!"

The three of them sat at the kitchen table with a sandwich, small avocado salad, and sweetened iced tea. Andy soon discovered that the attractive, blonde Mrs. Bing was fun. She had a good sense of humor and made Andy feel completely welcomed into the Bing home.

While they chatted and ate, the countertop TV showed the mid-day news program. The volume, however, had been turned down while they had lunch.

Suddenly, Becky jumped up and stepped toward the TV to raise the volume control. A news segment related to the recent Peck's Pond murder was being broadcast. The three of them turned their focus to the small screen.

"Earlier today, the North Haven Police held a press conference. We now bring you a tape of that session. Let's see what they had to say," the young, African-American female news anchor said.

The Chief of Police once again stood in front of several microphones.

"I want to report that we have now identified the murder victim found recently at Peck's Pond. The victim's name is Richard Baker. According to information provided by the FBI, Mr. Baker had been involved with illegal drug crimes for many years. He was thirty-two years old and has had several prior arrests.

"Now that we know the victim's identity, we are looking for a drug-related suspect in this murder. Also, based on expert forensic work, we are now confident the victim was not murdered at the pond site, but had been killed elsewhere then submerged into the swampy pond..

"Mr. Baker is not from this area. But according to the federal authorities, he had a recent residence in Houston, Texas. Our investigation, working with the FBI and the Connecticut State Detectives Unit, will continue until a suspect is found."

The film clip ended and the broadcaster reappeared.

"Well, in a way, that's good news! The murder wasn't linked to any students or staff," Mrs. Bing commented.

Becky muted the TV. Both teens sat quietly finishing their lunch after hearing the surprising news report. Still without a word, they climbed the stairs and darted into Becky's bedroom. She turned on the overhead fan as they both plopped down on the edge of her bed.

Andy broke the silence. "Hey, what the hell's going on? What is that bullshit we just heard on the news? That police report doesn't make sense. I mean, it's freakin' bogus. It's all screwed up!"

"Hmm. Yeah, I'm still thinking about it. So, maybe Jack, or this ah...Richard Baker, whoever the hell he was, had been a big drug dealer. We both know they were making pills in that underground factory."

"Yeah, but we both heard Miss Lakely call him by his first name. And that name was clearly 'Jack.' There's no mistake about that," said Andy.

"But, 'Jack' might have just been an alias or a nickname for this dude. And, maybe he didn't want Miss Lakely to know his real name. Or, maybe he was just running from the law and went by the name, Jack. I mean, hell, the possibilities are endless."

"Yeah, but we just heard that the FBI told the North Haven cops he came from Houston, Texas. And yet, we both heard Jack say he wanted to finish this job here right away to get back home to Chicago. And….there was something else. Do you remember when Miss Lakely was away from school that week? Mr. Pratt told our class she was out because she had personal things to take care of—back in Chicago."

There was a lull in the conversation as the two of them fell back, side by side, onto Becky's bedspread. They both stared up at the whirring fan without saying a word for several minutes.

"Andy, do you really believe that Miss Lakely is the murderer?" Another silent pause.

"Of course I don't know the answer to that but my gut tells me no. And, I know you saw a pistol in her shoulder bag. And we both saw the two of them together in that drug mill. But I just can't believe she is a killer. She…she just doesn't seem the type to be involved with murder and crimes and all that crap," he said.

"I know. I feel the same way. But maybe it's because you and I just like her so much. I mean, all the kids like her, not only as a teacher, but also as a cool human being. God, I wish we never saw her in the Hook Island factory building."

"You know, speaking of that place, Beck, what if our mystery man with the pinky ring in the video is good, ol' Mr. Barry Jones? That makes another connection to our school. Think about this. The teacher who got fired must somehow know of his replacement teacher, Miss Lakely."

"I know. And we really know nothing about that creepy, Neanderthal man, Jones. We only had him for homeroom a few minutes in the morning and just before dismissal. But, we don't know much more about Miss Lakely, either. So, the question is—do they know each other? And if so, when did they meet? If they did know each other—was it before she got hired or after she took over his classes?" Becky wondered.

"Good question. But I just thought of something else. Remember that man's voice we overheard in the drug mill office? Remember he got pissed he couldn't find the laboratory key ring? Ah, that would be the same key ring I held in my hand."

Becky smiled. "Yeah, I remember."

"Well, he called someone immediately from his cell. We both thought the voice was familiar but neither of us could place it. Now, I'm sure that voice did belong to Mr. Jones. It was Jones's voice, all right. And, now I'm convinced that was him hiding in the shadows on our vid…ah, I mean, of course, Bumper's video."

Becky turned her head to face her friend.

"And Andy, do you remember what subject Mr. Jones taught? Chemistry. He was obviously knowledgeable about working in a laboratory. In fact, if I remember, during our first few days of school and getting to know that creepy guy, he told us he had worked for a pharmaceutical company before teaching."

Andy popped up from the bed and grabbed Becky's laptop. He quickly accessed the Google Search window and keyed in "Amanda Lakely." There was only one match found. But that was the current Faculty Directory listing at North Haven High School.

"We gotta find answers about our mystery teacher, Miss Lakely," he said. "You know, things like where the hell did she come from and what did she do before coming to North Haven? That might lead us to her connection to our unemployed Chemistry teacher, Barry Jones."

Becky was pleased to see her boyfriend had not completely given up on the mystery.

"Andy, let's try her name again but qualify it within Chicago, or within the state of Illinois."

Andy launched the new search, but there was no match found. He turned for a long, serious look at Becky.

"You know what? I just thought about something. Just like Jack is not Richard Baker. I don't think that's her real name, Beck. I bet Amanda Lakely is some alias."

"Hey, I have an idea! We can look her up in the personnel files in the office tomorrow. And while we're at it, let's see if we can find anything on that creepy bastard, Mr. Jones."

The next morning brought lower humidity with a refreshing, cool, air mass blanketing Southern Connecticut. It was the first comfortable day in North Haven in weeks.

The summer school students reflected the change in weather with a renewed level of energy. They demonstrated this rejuvenation with excited chatter as they entered the school building. The summer program was now already into the second half of its term and would end soon. This contributed to the escalated energy.

When all five students were seated in Miss Lakely's Logic class, she stood before them and offered a proposal.

"Hey, guys, since today is so nice, why don't we change our venue? Let's hold our class outside so we can all enjoy this brilliant summer day rather than sacrifice it inside this stuffy classroom."

"Yeah, now you're talking, Miss Lakely," Hans responded with his high pitched voice. His wide opened eyes also reflected his approval of his teacher's outfit on this fine summer day. A small, navy-blue tank top with spaghetti straps emphasized her sexy figure. Her short pair of khaki shorts again exposed well-shaped and tanned legs. She boosted her body up onto the desk, which served as her seat, and faced the students.

"So, where can we all take a walk that's not too far away? Let's pick a spot where we can hold our group

154

discussion! I was thinking about the picnic tables at the shady side of the school building, or perhaps we could take a walk to the football stadium and have class in the stands," the teacher suggested in her perky tone.

The students all seemed agreeable to both venues, but Tyler Farnham trumped those with his own suggestion.

"How about we just cross the street and go over to Peck's Park, Miss Lakely? We could sit inside the town gazebo and have class there!" he recommended in his deep voice.

"Yeah, that's a great idea! I like it! Let's all go to Peck's Park," Hans said.

Amber, Becky, and Andy nodded in agreement.

"But, Peck's Park...that's ah...that's kind of close to Peck's Pond isn't it?" Miss Lakely asked with a noticeable anxiety in her voice. Silence filled the classroom.

Becky shot a glance at Andy, catching his attention. They both sensed their teacher wasn't too excited about holding an outside class session near Peck's Pond. It was the first time she publicly mentioned the crime scene.

But they were the only two who guessed why Miss Lakely might not want to return to the crime scene. Only the two of them knew the connection she had with the biker who had his life ended with a bullet through his head, and then was dumped into Peck's Pond.

"Oh no, Miss Lakely! Tyler responded, standing up by his desk. "We'll just go over to the far end of the park to the gazebo. There are barrier shrubs and trees that separate the park from the pond," he added with persuasive encouragement.

"Yeah, yeah, yeah, let's go," the students ratified.

Within fifteen minutes the teacher and her five students had assembled out at the town's public gazebo.

In the aftermath of the recent Independence Day parade and festivities, red white and blue bunting still hung around the structure. Several flower pots held vibrant, multi-colored petunias. The summer breeze provided a light, sweet fragrance for the students while they sat at random spots around the hexagonal wooden deck.

"Okay, so today I want to do something very different from our previous class sessions," the teacher began. "As I told you earlier, you're all getting advanced college credit for this course. And I promised I'd treat each of you like college students. So I thought for today's session, we'd not reference the internet sources or our class notes. I want our discussion to be personal and extemporaneous. Today, let's hear from anyone who'd like to relate, in your own life experience, with any of the Logic topics we've discussed in the past few weeks. We've covered a lot of material in a short time, but I want to hear what strikes you as perhaps the most important lesson learned."

"Ah, do you mean like experiencing things where we've seen people ASSUME something and come to a wrong conclusion before finding out the truth?" Becky asked.

Andy shot a fiery glare over to his girlfriend, who leaned back against the gazebo's balustrade. He guessed she was referring to the first day he had met her Caucasian mother at the Bing home.

"Yeah, Becky, that's one example. But I want you to also think about the consequences. In other words, what might have happened if the assumption wasn't used? How would good logical thinking have changed things?"

Tyler Farnham quickly raised his hand, anxious to speak. "Miss Lakely, I've been thinking a lot about something we discussed in class. It goes back to that day you wrote on the board. You know, that expression, 'Things are not always what they seem to be.' And I think there's something all of us in this class can all relate to with that anonymous proverb."

"Yes, supposedly that expression was coined several centuries ago by the ancient Chinese spiritual leader,

Lao Tze. He, as some of you might know, is the creator of Taoism philosophy," commented Miss Lakely.

"Yeah, well, I've thought about it and actually found many instances in my life where that old axiom has been true. But the most recent example and the one that affects all of us in this school is what I want to talk about today," Tyler said.

The comment triggered an escalated interest level and the teacher and students now turned to focus on the popular and handsome, Tyler Farnham.

"Well, your introduction is very intriguing. Let's hear about it, Tyler! I'm sure you've got something interesting to tell all of us," Miss Lakely said, as she turned to the others sitting around the gazebo. "And when Tyler's finished, I'd like to see each of you come up and relate something you learned in our class with your own personal experience."

Tyler slowly raised himself up from the gazebo decking. His hands lightly brushed off stone-washed cargo shorts. He chose to stand in a shaded spot to avoid the rising sun glaring directly into his eyes. After clearing his throat, he addressed the small group of peers. Today he appeared uncharacteristically anxious—more emotionally charged than usual.

"Just a few weeks ago, we...we felt a very deep and personal loss. For some of us, this loss turned to grief. It happened right after we learned of Cindy's tragic death The news struck all of us personally whether we were close to Cindy or hardly knew her at all.

"I've been a next-door neighbor to the Shea family for all my life. I've been close friends with Cindy since elementary school. I can tell you from a personal perspective that she was one helluva terrific person! I was always just one year behind Cindy; in school, Little League, CCD, track, and even the Young Republicans Club. Despite our year's difference in age, we were close, very close. And I probably know her better than any other kid in this town."

Tyler paused as his voice weakened. He needed to take in a deep breath to prepare for an emotional storm swelling within him.

"But I was especially troubled by the public reports of how poor Cindy had died." He once again cleared his throat. "I know you all heard the stories. I'm sure you all read the headlines, but then the stories continued beyond the accident. Stories of how Cindy was under the influence of drugs when she drove her car off of the road.

"And this is where I tie my story and…and my personal hurt, into this Logic class lesson—things aren't always as they seem. Because, it wasn't what *was* reported in the media. It's what *wasn't* reported in the media.

"First, as I told you, I KNEW Cindy Shea. I KNEW everything about her. Her passion was school, sports and taking care of her little brother who is developmentally challenged. She was always a happy girl. Cindy was a responsible and level-headed individual. And, I can tell you, she was the sweetest, most compassionate girl you'd ever meet. Doing drugs or alcohol was NEVER, NEVER in her personal sphere of being. It just wasn't part of her life. She never had time for that and knew full well the risk and the consequences of driving a car under the influence. I'm telling you, all of you, Cindy Shea would never have done such an irresponsible thing!"

Tyler took another deep breath, while the students and teacher sat frozen, concentrating on his every word.

"But…but the rumors and typical gossip buzz continued. Some were painfully wrong like calling her just another wild teenager, partying during high school graduation week. Or, I heard comments like, 'it's sad that the young girl made a bad decision', or worst of all, 'maybe that will be a lesson to others young kids', et cetera, et cetera.

"You see, these people are the uneducated or narrow-minded assholes who always ignore the

158

expression that Miss Lakely wrote on the board. 'Things are not always as they seem.'

"And I'll share with all of you this morning what I just learned from her family. Mr. and Mrs. Shea told me the detailed toxicology report from the Medical Examiner's office included much more than what was in the press. And that report was professional and objective. It wasn't salacious media bullshit that drove people into knee-jerk assumptions. And what I'm going to tell you underscores how the media often reports information that is far from the proven truth."

Miss Lakely, with arms folded, listened to the young man's diatribe. The other four students now moved around, anxiously awaiting Tyler's revelation of something important, something climactic. But without exception, they all respected his integrity and his courage to take control of the class to tell his story.

He took in a deep breath and exhaled before continuing. "Those drugs found in Cindy's body were recreational hallucinogens all right, but they were not party drugs. The drugs were nasty chemicals typically administered when the victim doesn't know about them.

"The forensic detectives told Cindy's father about the drugs found inside of her. And Mr. Shea told me about them just last night. They were Gammahydroxybutrate, Ketamine, and Rohypnol—. 'roofies.' Do you all know what these are?"

Tyler paused and then continued.

"Well, they're commonly known as 'date-rape' drugs. Yeah, I said 'date-rape' drugs. Usually only one of these compounds is slipped into some girl's drink at a party. But in Cindy's case, she wasn't at any party as far as we know. And, in her case a new combination of all three substances was used. And…and was she raped? Yes, she was raped!" he yelled out, facing his classmates.

The students shifted in uncomfortable anxiety. They listened as Tyler's voice shook and became louder with emotion. After pausing again, he continued.

"Her father told me that also. There was clear evidence of sexual contact before she was killed. But the Shea family, especially her mother, didn't want any of this to come out in the media. They were distraught enough. They knew their daughter wasn't coming back to them, so they just let it go. They had to let it go. The Shea family didn't care about the details of poor Cindy's accident. Or, should I say, poor Cindy's murder."

The students seemed to recoil at the word *murder*.

"Because I knew Cindy, I know that she'd want others to know the truth. She wouldn't care about her own reputation, but she'd want the truth to be known to warn other teens who could become victims of date-rape drugs."

Tyler inhaled and exhaled slowly once again, trying to release his pent-up emotion.

"So what has all this got to do with this Logic class? Well, we learned early that to be good diagnosticians or detectives, we must never take things at face value, and never come to conclusions without the proven facts. It goes back to the expression—things are not always what they seem to be.

"So, if any of you hear that Cindy Shea's life had ended in vain, or she was partying during her last week of high school, just don't believe any of it! But remember—things are not always what they seem to be."

The students watched in silence as Tyler's face wrenched up into a painful expression and his eyes welled up with tears. Now it seemed he couldn't look directly at his teacher or any of his classmates. Without warning, he marched straight ahead and stepped off of the gazebo steps. He kept walking away from them without ever looking back.

Those remaining were dumbstruck. They remained motionless and silent for several moments, with the exception of Amber Woods, who tried to stifle her sobbing but was unsuccessful.

160

A ring tone from someone's cell phone jolted the students and Miss Lakely out of their subdued trance. The sound came from inside Miss Lakely's straw shoulder bag. It sat on the deck next to where Andy sat with his legs folded Indian style.

Andy reached over, grabbed the bag, and then stood up, handing it to his teacher.

"Thank you, Andy," she said softly.

Miss Lakely rose up and strutted away from the students as she plucked the cell out the straw bag. Turning away from the group she faced the far reaches of Peck's Park. She then spoke in a low, nearly inaudible tone.

"Yeah, what's up?" She then paused to listen to the caller. "Sure. No problem. We're about wrapped up here for now anyway."

Amanda Lakely snapped the cell phone shut. She turned around to now face the four students. After taking in a deep breath and exhaling, she spoke to the teens.

"Okay. I think we've all learned something today. In fact, I've personally learned a hell of a lot. And with the raw nerves and emotions of this morning, I think it best to cut the class off right here. Besides, that was Mr. Pratt who just called. He seemed quite upset that we held our class outdoors so close to Peck's Pond. So, we'd have to finish our class session inside the school. But I don't think any of us wants to do that now. So let's call it a day. I think we're finished with reality experiences. We'll move on to our next topic during our next class."

The group then split up, going in different directions. Miss Lakely hustled back toward the school. Becky and Andy followed slowly behind, neither speaking a word. Although they didn't want to work now, they had promised Mrs. Savoyski they'd help out in the main office that morning. They stopped by the vending machine to pick up a cold bottle of water before crossing the threshold into the office with the small brass sign—"Administration."

Mr. Savoyski greeted the teens with her typical smile. "Oh, hello, kids! You're a little early today, but that's a good thing! I have lots for you to do and I must leave a little early this afternoon."

"Sure, but what do you need done?" Becky asked.

"Well, the other day I showed you how to read the class schedules on the Power School© computer program. But as you can imagine, there are always changes coming in with kids coming and leaving the school. So now, I have changes and updates to be made to the scheduling data. Maybe if you, Becky, enter the changes and 'add-ons' into the system from the input forms, Andy can then file each of the hard copies into the student's folders. Then we'll have the current schedule for each student online and a back-up hard copy. That's how we always do it and the process works well."

The experienced administrator led Andy to a long oak table adjacent to the file cabinets.

"Now, Andy, here is the list of students' names for whom we need to change schedules. You can pull their file folders and insert the latest schedule page. They're in alphabetical order. Then you must initial the sign-off box on the outside of each student's folder. This indicates that you were the last person to open the student folder with an official update to the contents."

Andy acknowledged the process. Then his eyes scanned the outside of some of the folders. There were columns with dates and initials from previous updates.

"Oh, Mrs. Savoyski, I see the initials of 'AW' on some of the student folders. I bet those were from Amber Woods, am I right?"

"Huh? Oh, yes, yes it is. Amber was such a great worker! She only lasted a week, but she was such a big help to me, just as I'm sure you two will turn out to be."

Andy's fingers flipped through some of the folders in the drawer. He pulled out a handful of them. He saw the initials 'CS' written on columns with a date earlier in the school year.

"Say, who belongs to the initials 'CS', Mrs. Savoyski? I see that person had initialed a lot of these folders."

There was a long pause before she managed to answer.

"Oh, 'CS', yes...yes, that...that was Cindy Shea." She seemed to stare into space. "Poor Cindy, I...I just can't get over what happened to her. It is just so sad. She was the best! She was the most reliable student I ever had help me inside of this office. Poor Cindy, she was such a sweet, sweet girl!"

Becky's head swiveled around from the computer screen. But her silent glare wasn't aimed at Mrs. Savoyski. It was focused directly at Andy Abbot.

He returned the stare silently acknowledging the new coincidences being revealed. The rest of the morning went smoothly with Andy and Becky performing their administrative tasks independently. At noon, Mrs. Savoyski approached the two of them with a large brass ring of keys in her hand.

"Here, before I forget, I want to show you where I keep the keys. I'll be in later tomorrow morning, quite some time after you two arrive. I have to stop at the *New Haven Register* and submit a press release."

Mrs. Savoyski looked around the office then whispered to the two junior students. "I'll let you two in on some gossip a little early. There'll be an article in Sunday's newspaper. Mr. Pratt is announcing his retirement. It came on all of a sudden. Nobody expected it, especially me. He told me yesterday he'll stay around for the remainder of the summer but he's not returning in September. I'm sure going to miss him."

"Wow, that is news!" said Andy. "My older brother had Mr. Pratt several years ago when he attended school here. So, the silver fohhhh...ah, Mr. Pratt's been around for a while."

"Oh...yes. And I've worked for Mr. Pratt now almost eight years. But, he's also trained our two Assistant Principals well. Either one can fill in easily for him. So, I'm sure there'll be no glitches until the school board hires a new principal."

The older woman winked then changed topics.

"Anyway, this key ring is always hung inside the coat closet over there. I'll give it to you now so you two can lock up before you leave for the day. Tomorrow, just unlock the file cabinet and you can finish this class schedule project. I'll probably be in around noontime. Now, Mr. Pratt is gone for the rest of today, but he'll be up at his cabin now. If there is an emergency of any kind you can call me or contact him up at Bantam Lake. The numbers are on the Rolodex on my desk."

Mr. Savoyski handed the key ring to Becky then locked up her own desk and was soon gone from the office. After she was outside of earshot, Andy commented to Becky.

"God, this is so creepy seeing Cindy Shea's initials on the student folders. I mean, just after hearing Tyler tell his story about her this morning. And now seeing her handwriting on the cover makes me feel a little...a little weird."

Becky looked down at the key ring in her hand. There had to be a dozen keys hanging from it. She fingered each key individually inspecting the make and wondering what each might be used for.

"I know, Andy. I'm still blown away at what Tyler told us. There is just too much weird crap going on around her drug death, Amber's drug-rape and our school. Everything is whirling around in my brain but I can't put it all together. It makes me dizzy just thinking about everything. There's a ..."

Becky stopped mid-sentence and sat quietly staring into space.

"There's a what, Becky?"

"There's a jigsaw puzzle sitting in front of you and me and we can't seem to make any of the damn pieces fit together."

"And don't forget Mr. Jones, or at least we're pretty sure it was Mr. Jones in the dark tunnel at Hook Island. If that was him, what the hell was he doing there in the darkness? And we heard him in the same office we had earlier discovered Miss Lakely. This is so freakin' mind boggling!"

"C'mon...let's see if we can find something out about Mr. Barry Jones and maybe something about Miss Lakely."

"Huh?"

She raised the key ring into the air.

"Let's find the key to the file cabinet that holds all the faculty members' folders."

They soon found the beige metal file cabinet labeled "Faculty." Within minutes, one of Mrs. Savoyski's keys opened the metal drawer. Becky quickly thumbed through the faculty folders until she came to the end. There was no folder labeled "Jones." There was a separate section of folders for "Past Faculty" members. They slowly scanned through the names on that group of folders. Again the search was unsuccessful. There were none labeled with his name. They silently searched a second time with no luck.

"That's really weird. Mr. Jones was obviously one of the past faculty members, but he has no folder."

"Hey Becky, let's go back to Miss Lakely's file. Let's see what we can learn about the mystery linked to that chick."

Becky stopped looking at the folders and raised her head to stare into Andy's eyes.

"That chick? What...what the hell's this about our teacher being called...that chick?"

Andy suddenly felt uncomfortable and felt his face flush with embarrassment.

"I...I don't know. My God, it's just an expression. C'mon, c'mon, let's find her folder."

She thumbed through until she came to the folder labeled "Lakely, Amanda." She quickly pulled it out of the drawer and opened it on the desk behind her.

There were only a few pieces of paper inside the teacher's folder. One was a copy of her certification to teach secondary education within the State of Connecticut. Behind that was her computer-printed resume.

"Hey, look at this, Becky! Miss Lakely graduated from Ohio State University just a few years ago."

"Yeah, I see that. But there doesn't seem to be anything unusual with that. It looks like she majored in Math with a minor in Chemistry. Hmm…Chemistry, isn't that interesting. She could probably teach Chemistry, just like Mr. Jones did last year. So if she knew Chemistry, she'd also be capable of working in a lab, mixing chemical compounds."

Andy only stared at his friend, the movement of his Adam's apple revealing a silent gulp. His nightmare about the disjointed, dangerous, and real-life puzzle was returning.

They returned the folder to the cabinet, disappointed at not finding any more clues. Andy paced around inside the school's main office. He then stopped in his steps. He had an epiphany.

"You know what, Beck? We can't put the pieces of this puzzle together because we're drowning in too much information. We have a lot of data, but we're missing one important thing."

"Oh, we're missing one thing? Now, pray tell, what's that, Andy?"

"It's called logic. Remember what Miss Lakely told us, that how in real life, the detectives, doctors and others use a white board to help analyze the facts and develop some sound logic associated with the information they've found. They often draw a diagram and visually link those data together. So, that's what you and I need to do. We need to link all of this information into some logical and orderly form. It will show us the relationships and give us some clues. C'mon, let's go!"

"But…but where are we going?"

"We'll go to my house. I have one of those big white boards upstairs."

"Now, why doesn't that surprise me?" Becky joked.

CHAPTER SIXTEEN

Mrs. Abbot greeted the two teens as they arrived at the house. For a few moments the three sat on the front porch rocking on the chairs and casually chatting about school. While doing so, Andy got an incoming text message from Bumper Stone.

Becky told Mrs. Abbot about their part-time work assignment in the North Haven School office and how she enjoyed working with the affable Mrs. Savoyski.

Andy interrupted their conversation.

"Oh my God, this is funny," Andy said looking at the text message on his cell phone screen. He chuckled as he kept his eyes focused on the text.

"What? What's new with our good buddy, Bumper?" Becky asked with a hint of sarcasm.

"Yes. How are Bumper and his mom doing?" Mrs. Abbot asked.

"Well, it seems he and some of his New York City friends scored some wine and beer the other night. A bunch of them went to a city park and drank the booze and ate pizza. They had their own summer party goin' on. But of course, Bumper overindulged and got terribly sick. He says he puked all night long and had a hangover that lasted for two days. Ha! He now says he is swearing off booze for the rest of his life!"

Mrs. Abbot chuckled. "Well, maybe that's a good thing, swearing off booze, especially for a sixteen-year-old."

"Yeah, but what he really has to swear off is eating pizza. He'll never give that up!"

The three of them laughed together before Andy led Becky upstairs. But he took a quick detour into his older brother's bedroom. He soon came out rolling a huge white board with its frame on rubber wheels.

"My God, Andy! That white board is enormous! What is it for?" Becky asked.

"Oh, my parents got it for my brother and me when we were little. We used to play tic-tac-toe on it and other goofy games. We'd draw, and later we all used it for Pictionary games and stuff like that. But now, this old white board is a tool for our logic brainstorming session. Remember what Miss Lakely told us about 'House" and 'Cold Case' and other shows? The main characters all get together and talk about what they know and if it seems important, they jot it down on the board."

"Yeah, that's right! So, why don't we start with a time-line? We'll draw it at the top of the board."

Becky grabbed a blue marker and drew a horizontal date line. Andy then added in green the events that occurred, beginning with the discovery of Miss Lakely and Jack the Biker at the underground office. Following this, Becky added Jack's murdered body found at Peck's Pond. Andy's marker then went to the beginning of the time-line adding "Mr. Jones at New Age jamming session." Next was the discovery of the drug laboratory. Becky added the phrase "Amber Woods drugged."

Andy noticed that Becky didn't write the word "drug-rape" onto the white board. But the addition onto the timeline made him consider something. He added "Mr. Pratt" under Amber's name with a slanted line coming down from the drugging event. Then he added another slanted line coming further down the board with the phrase "motorcycle sound" with question marks.

"Hey, Beck, I just thought of something. When we're finished brainstorming here with our decision tree, we'd better cover up our work. I don't want my mom to see this information. It'll freak her out."

Becky nodded. "We'll pin up some material over the board." Andy continued with the time line inserting the phrase "Miss Lakely doesn't come forward" under the 'Jack the Biker' murder phrase.

The two stopped for a moment and sat on Andy's bed, staring at their notes. Becky suddenly turned to grab Andy's notebook computer. She tapped in a few commands and pulled up the website for Ohio State University. As she did so, Andy added more to the time line. After a few minutes, Becky turned to face him.

"You can add one more item to the board, Andy."

"Oh? What is that?"

"Miss Lakely never attended Ohio State University. She is not recorded as a graduate in that year as listed in her resume. I also just checked other years but her name is not on any of the university's graduating rosters. I don't think she ever went to Ohio State."

"Hmm. So our teacher continues to be a mystery woman. I really doubt her real name is Amanda Lakely. I bet she's using an alias, just like our murder victim, Jack."

Andy stood up and added those notes to the white board. The two stared at their work once again.

"That's helpful, but I think we have to add something at the very beginning of our time-line."

"Huh? Add what?"

Becky stood up, taking the colored marker from his hand. She then approached the board and carefully wrote the phrase at the very beginning of the time line—"Cindy Shea drugged/killed."

"Geez, Beck, do you really think Cindy's accident and…and death is connected to all of this crap? I mean, I know we heard a lot from Tyler. And, it was very emotional. But all we know is that she had some nasty drugs on board during that car accident."

"But it's just too damn coincidental! They found her body full of date-rape drugs. Tyler implied very convincingly that those drugs were given to her without her knowing it. You heard him. Cindy was not a party girl. She would never take drugs!"

"So how...how does her death link to all of this?"

There was a momentary pause before Becky turned and wrote once again on the white board. "CS worked in school office." Then she wrote under Amber Woods name on the board: "AW worked in school office."

Andy watched as Becky drew a line connecting the two students: one recently deceased through drugs and one allegedly raped through drugs.

"So, if both girls worked part time in the office, there is a person who connects the two of them."

"Oh, God! You're talking about 'the old silver fox', Mr. Pratt, right?"

"Of course! Listen! Mr. Pratt knew both of them, and got to know them more closely after they worked in the office. We don't know about his relationship with Cindy, but we do know how he became chummy with Amber. We also know he lured her up to his cabin at Bantam Lake and probably drugged her."

Becky put away her marker then allowed her body to collapse onto Andy's bed. She stared up at the bedroom ceiling fan without saying a word. Finally, she broke the silence.

"Andy, I've been playing back our class session at the gazebo in my head. I've an important question for you."

"Yeah, what is it?"

"When Miss Lakely's cell phone rang this morning, you grabbed her straw shoulder bag and handed it to her. I saw her take the bag from you but then she turned to take out the cell. From where I was sitting, I couldn't see what she did or hear what she said."

"Yeah, so where are you going with this?"

"Well, after she finished the conversation, she snapped the cell phone shut and put it back inside her bag. Then she turned to face us once again, telling us it was Mr. Pratt who had called. She told us that Pratt was pissed about our class session outside, near Peck's Pond."

"Yeah, so what? So what's your question for me?"

"Andy, you were the closest person to Miss Lakely during that call. Did she use her red iPhone when she answered the call?"

"Huh? Ah…no, it wasn't that cool red cell she picked out of her bag. It was a…."

"Dark blue cell phone," she interrupted.

"You mean the same cell…."

"Yes!" Becky said. "It was the same cell phone she used when we spied on her inside the drug mill at Hook Island."

"So you're saying when Mr. Pratt and she talked on the cell, he called her on that blue phone and not on her personal one." Andy thought about the coincidence. "Do you think it was 'the old, silver fox' who spoke with Miss Lakely that day on the island? And remember, that was the same day she had been with Jack the Biker."

"It could have been Pratt on the phone. We may never find out. But if it was Jack, aka Richard Baker, he may have known Pratt, too. The conversation was about Jack and his getting out of control. The three of them were into some sort of ring and they communicated with the blue cell phone number."

"You know, I think you're onto something, Beck. The three of them, and perhaps Barry Jones, were together in some sort of underground crime ring."

Becky stood up from the bed. She gathered the markers and approached the white board once more. She now drew a line connecting Miss Lakely with Mr. Pratt who was already linked to Amber and the deceased Cindy Shea.

But Andy saw one more missing link. He took the marker from Becky's hand. In large capital letters he wrote next to Miss Lakely's, "CARRIES A PISTOL."

Now they both stepped back to look at their work. In silence, they reviewed the times, the names, and the phrases.

Several bright colored lines crisscrossed the white board connecting names and data. From a distance it looked like a complex network of telecommunication lines. But as they stared at their work, there were no brainstorms popping up.

"Just looking at all this stuff gives me a headache," Andy commented. Becky looked over at him with a smile that turned into giggle.

"What's so funny?" Andy asked, a little irritated.

"It's your nose! It has green magic marker all over it!"

Andy ambled over to his dresser mirror. He immediately saw the green smudge over the tip of his nose. Realizing how silly he looked, he turned and smiled at Becky now sitting on the bed. As he approached her, he picked the red marker from her grasp.

"So, if I look like a clown with a green colored nose, I think it only fitting that you should look the same. Only you'll have a nice big, red clown nose!"

He then lunged toward her on top of the bed. Becky fell back again, her body bouncing on the mattress. She turned her head to the side and screamed, "Oh, no, no you wouldn't dare!"

Andy quickly straddled her petite body with both of his long legs. He pinned her hands down on top of the bedspread. With one hand Andy held her face in place while he lightly swabbed her nose with bright red marker.

"Oh, you son of a..."

But Andy cut her off before she could continue speaking. He quickly lowered his face down to hers. Her head stopped moving as she gave in to his gentle, tender kiss. As their moist lips met, their noses touched; his green, hers red.

While kissing, they embraced, each feeling the warmth of the other's body.

His arms slipped underneath the small of her back. With one fluid motion he rolled onto his back picking her body up as he did so. She now ended up on top of his body, her lips still locked with his.

They finally broke apart. Heavy breathing made their chests heave in unison. Becky, now lying on top of her boyfriend, traced his face with her fingertips, and then lowered her lips once more to taste Andy's sweet mouth.

But this kiss had more hunger. It was forceful, sensuous and exploring. A soft moaning sound came from Becky as she pulled him closer to her. The message it carried was not lost on the young man. He became aroused with her sensuality.

Suddenly, the mood was broken. Mrs. Abbot's footsteps could be heard stepping up the oak staircase.

Becky and Andy quickly jumped up from the bed.

"Andy, quick—let's cover up the white board!" Becky whispered.

Andy turned and looked for something to cover up their brainstorming work. He stepped over to his closet and pulled out a linen bedcover. Becky helped him drape the material over the white board. Just as they pulled it down, Mrs. Abbot stopped just outside the bedroom door.

CHAPTER SEVENTEEN

"K nock, knock," Mrs. Abbot politely called out just before she turned the doorknob and opened the bedroom door. The forty-something woman stood at the threshold staring at her son and his first girlfriend. The two teens tried to hide their nervous surprise at her sudden appearance.

"Oh, hi, Mom! What's up?" Andy stood at one side of the covered white board while Becky positioned herself guarding the opposite end.

"Well! It looks like you two are protecting some top-secret project there. What is it, something to do with your summer Logic course?"

"Yeah, as a matter of fact it is, Mrs. Abbot," Becky replied. "It's something we need to work on together, analyzing a problem. I figured if it was covered, Andy wouldn't work on it by himself until I return to help him with it."

Andy peered over at his cute girlfriend who stood smiling with composure. He was once again amazed at how she could think so quickly on her feet—literally, and still without outright lying to his mother.

"Aha! Good idea, Becky. But you might want to staple or tape that bedspread to the board so he's not tempted to sneak at it while he's alone up here."

"Yeah, I think I just might do that, Mrs. Abbot!" Becky glanced over at Andy meeting his face with a wink.

"Becky, I stopped by to ask you to stay for dinner with us tonight. We're just going to grill some steaks outside with some potato salad. We'd love to have you join us if you can."

Becky responded with a smile. "I'd love to, Mrs. Abbot. I'll call my folks and let them know."

"That would be great, but the two of you should listen to me. I have some very good advice for the both of you," Mrs. Abbot admonished.

Andy's face quickly turned to a crimson red, anticipating an embarrassing comment.

"What, what's that, Mom?" he asked nervously.

"Before dinner, don't forget to wash up. And my advice to you is that you should both wash off those clown noses. " She winked and smiled at them as she reached for the doorknob. She shut the door behind her and was soon heard stepping down the staircase.

Andy walked over to Becky and placed both of his hands on her soft shoulders.

"Thanks, Becky," was followed by a light peck on the lips. She smiled and held his hand. They both slid the white board to one side of the room. The brainstorming session had exhausted them.

They spent the remainder of the afternoon outside in the Abbot driveway, shooting baskets. Later, they walked around the Beechwood Knoll neighborhood— hand in hand.

* * *

Later, after Mr. Abbot arrived home, the four of them talked golf while they ate dinner. The discussion ended with a commitment that they'd all go out for a round of eighteen holes in the near future.

Mr. and Mrs. Abbot stayed drinking coffee, while the two teens offered to clean up. When they were alone in the kitchen, rinsing dishes at the sink, Andy stopped what he was doing.

He leaned over and whispered to Becky with a fiery sense of urgency in his eyes.

"You know what I think, Beck? I think you and I have to go back upstairs into my bedroom."

Becky looked into his eyes to decipher what was on his mind. With their hands submerged under the sink's sudsy water, she let her fingers wander to find his larger hand. Her fingertips crawled sensuously along the back of one of his soapy hands.

"Oh? Did you have something on your mind?" Becky whispered with a seductive smile.

"Yeah, as a matter of fact, I do," he answered softly looking into her eyes.

"I'm ready whenever you are."

The two dried off their hands and strolled out to the patio as his parents finished their coffee.

"Thank you for dinner, Mr. and Mrs. Abbot. I really enjoyed it!"

"Oh, you're welcome, Becky," replied Mrs. Abbot. "And thank you for helping with the dishes. Hey, we're going out for some Dairy Queen pretty soon. Do you two want to come along?"

"Ah, I don't think so, Mom. Becky and I have just a little more to do on our project for tonight. Then I'm going to walk her back to her house. Thanks anyway!"

The two then turned around and quickly jogged up the staircase, this time Becky leading Andy. After they were both inside the bedroom, Andy closed the door.

The two of them just stood there inside the bedroom without saying a word. Their hearts now pounded with intensity.

With his eyes still riveted onto hers, Andy outstretched his arm, grabbed the doorknob, and turned the inner lever, locking the bedroom door. Becky's eyes swiveled to watch what he did. A warm smile lit up his face.

"Becky, I got to tell you, I'm impressed with the way you're always thinking ahead. I mean, I really admire how you warned me about taking precautions!

Now, Mom or Dad can't barge in! We'll have to unlock it for them and that will give us time to cover up the white board. So, now let's get into why I wanted us back up here." Andy stepped toward the far end of the room, leaving Becky standing alone by the door.

"Becky, at dinner tonight, I thought about some key stuff we had omitted in our analysis…ah, our logic."

She smiled as her friend enthusiastically picked up a marker. He turned, waiting for her to get into gear once again.

"C'mon, Beck, we still got work to do here," he said. Becky slowly stepped forward, joining him on the side of the bed facing their time line of events written in multiple colored lines and notations.

"First of all, if we're going to add Amber's creepy experience and possible rape…."

"Andy, the girl was raped," she interrupted. "Don't use the word, 'possible'. Amber knows what was done to her. She just doesn't know or…or remember, who did it to her." He quickly nodded in agreement while picking up the marker.

"Do you remember when I asked Amber about things she may have heard during or after the incident? She told us she only remembered bizarre images of some weird guy. But when I asked about sounds, she told us there was only one," Andy added.

"Yeah, she heard the loud sound of an engine, something like a motorcycle starting up."

"Right! She had said she heard it when she was coming to out of the drug induced coma. She was in and out of consciousness but could still hear the sound of a motorcycle."

"Well, Jack rode a bike. That may have been his bike that Amber heard outside of that Bantam Lake cabin," Andy said.

Becky pondered the emerging hypothesis.

"That might be a stretch, Andy. And we still don't have Pratt directly connected to Jack the Biker. Don't forget that happened back in April. We didn't know anything about Jack's existence until late June." Andy jotted the words 'motorcycle sounds' followed with question marks next to Amber's phrases.

"I'm saying there's a connection from the underground drug laboratory at Hook Island to Bantam Lake. And if Miss Lakely was talking to Mr. Pratt on the blue cell phone that day in the drug mill, Jack must have known our principal, too. I wonder if the three of them worked together somehow," Andy said.

"Hmm. You think it's possible that Pratt shot and killed the bike-man, Jack?"

"Hell, who knows? And don't forget, we only know Miss Lakely carries a gun in her handbag. We still don't know about Pratt having a weapon. I do remember the police reported that the biker was shot with a nine-millimeter gun. You don't happen to know what the gun looked like in Miss Lakely's bag, do you?"

"Huh? You gotta be kidding me! I don't know anything about guns. All I know is that I saw one in her straw bag," Becky said.

"You know, there's another loose end that I thought about earlier, Beck. We never found anything more on Mr. Jones. And I'm certain it was him lurking in the shadows of the creepy factory. He was snooping on New Age while they practiced. He's still a mystery."

"Well, there was no record of him in the file of terminated faculty members. No resumé, no application, not even any letters about him on file. But of course, Mr. Pratt could have taken care of disposing of that if they were in this together."

Becky lay backward across Andy's bed, looking up again at the ceiling fan circulating at a slow speed.

"What are you thinking about now, Beck?"

"You and I are soooo in over our heads trying to solve this mystery. I mean, we're looking at a complex case with one definite homicide and perhaps another potential murder of one of our classmates. Those date rape drugs from the underground lab might be connected to Cindy Shea's fatal accident. But we don't know how those drugs got into her or who gave them to her. And I'm still troubled by Amber's drug-induced rape up in Bantam Lake. We know Mr. Pratt has a role in this, but we aren't sure what the hell it is. Andy, I think it's time to go forward on this."

"You mean, go to the police?"

"Perhaps we should consider that."

"Now, Becky, you're making sense. This case is waaaaaay too big for two high school students to solve."

Becky continued to stare at the ceiling, never looking over at her friend.

"Yeah, but I was just thinking about a different approach to solving all this crap. I wonder what would happen if we confronted Miss Lakely first. You know, one last thread to follow before we go to the cops. We know she's involved, but still don't know how and why. We only saw her in the lab office that night with Jack who is now dead."

Andy raised his hand, his index finger pointing up to the white board. "Yeah, dead from a gunshot wound! Perhaps that gunshot came from the gun hidden inside Lakely's shoulder bag. She's got to be guilty of something with all this crap going on. How many school teachers pack a weapon in their handbag, for God's sake?"

"I don't know. But I'd like to at least confront her first before we go to the police."

"Geez, Beck, don't you think that's ah...a little freakin' risky? I mean, if she's into some drug ring, and maybe involved with Jack's murder, there's nothing to stop her from killing you and me. And after she finds out how much we know and we're still snooping around, what's to prevent her from using her gun on us?" Another pause while Becky thought about the risk.

"Well, maybe if we confront her in a public place and tell her we found out some things, before we go to the cops, we'll see how she reacts. If she's guilty of something or anything, it will show. If we do have this meeting with her, say in the library at school with others around us, there is no risk of her reacting. She won't pull out a gun inside a library."

"But what if she does react, gets pissed, and runs out of the library?"

"We'll call 911 and have the cops cut her off before her escape. We'll make the call before she makes it to the library door. The squad cars would be there within minutes."

"Hmm. I don't know about this, Beck. I mean up until now we...we've just made like this whole thing is like a game...like some kind of jigsaw puzzle. We kept finding more things that seemed at first disconnected and then tried to fit those pieces together. But...but now, we're deep into a serious life and death situation. And I think confronting...confronting someone who might be a murderer is dangerous. This is no game or some TV reality show. It's real life and it's our lives!"

"But, listen, what if she is innocent but involved. If she runs out because she is scared and if we go to the cops, the wrong person will get arrested. This gives the others, whoever they are, time to defend themselves. And you know what that means; there will be alibis, lawyers, and all that crap! The criminals will have time to set up defenses. And they'll all go completely free! We will have...have...fucked up the whole case. And you and I still don't have any actual evidence or proof of anything. Right now, all we know is that Miss Lakely's involved somehow. She's at the center of this thing but we don't know how exactly she fits in. Don't you see? Our teacher is the key piece to that jigsaw puzzle. Once we find out exactly her role, then we can go to the cops and report our findings. If she confesses, we'll have it on tape."

"On tape, what the hell are you thinking, Becky?"

"Well, if we're going to stage a showdown and ask her direct questions, we gotta have it on tape, or else we'll have nothing."

"Oh...Becky, for God's sake, she's not going to agree to a meeting with us in the library with a tape recorder going on."

"I know that! But you're gonna have a hidden microphone and recorder on you."

Andy grabbed one of the bed pillows and squashed it hard against is face. He needed to escape the madness and not listen to any more ideas how to figure this case out. After a few moments he tossed the pillow high into the air, letting it fall on the carpet. He lay still on his back not saying a word with his eyes closed.

Becky knew her boyfriend was anxious. Slowly, she turned on her side placing her hand lightly on his chest. She could feel a slight heaving up and down. Still with his eyes closed, Andy spoke. His voice didn't hide his anger and frustration.

"God! I wish I never got involved with all this shit. I never wanted to go to Hook Island that first night for that...that absentee asshole, Bumper. And I really wanted to take the AP Algebra course rather than this stupid, freakin' Logic class with Miss Lakely. Math is my thing, not this logical detective work that we got sucked into. Those two bad decisions got you and me into this...this freakin' murder and drug mystery. The whole thing is consuming us and...and ruining our summer."

Becky quietly grinned at him. She waited a moment before leaning over toward him. She kissed his lips softly, aware that his emotions were rattled with all they had been through.

After the tender kiss, Andy opened his eyes, realizing he was just acting out and displaying immaturity and self-pity.

"Can you walk me home now, Andy?"

He leaned over toward her and kissed her moist lips.

"Sure, let's go."

CHAPTER EIGHTEEN

The next morning was once again overcast with intermittent light showers. At nine, the students were all seated in their classrooms to begin the last few days of summer school. Colorful umbrellas lay at the rear of the classroom drying out. Despite the gloomy weather, Miss Lakely was still in her bubbly persona addressing the AP class.

"Today, class, I want each of you to take a half hour and write a brief paper. The purpose of the paper is to tell me what career you plan on pursuing over the next five to ten years. I don't need to know why or how you reached that decision, which we all know is subject to change several times over the near future. But the rest of your paper is to identify how you would need to use logic in the professional career you plan to pursue. I would like three detailed examples of how logic would be required in your job."

Hans Schmidt was the first to raise his hand.

"Yes, Hans, what is it?"

"For those of us who have our notebook computers or laptops with us, can we use them and print off our papers on the network printer?"

"Of course!" she replied.

"Cool!" Hans said.

"Now, when you've finished your paper, just walk to the office to get your document from the printer. I don't expect your composition to be more than one to two pages. Now remember, you only have thirty minutes to do this. And that brings me to the next part of today's class. I have the final test that I'll hand out to each of you after you turn in your paper. Your paper will be forty percent of your course grade, and the test will count towards the other sixty per cent of the grade. While you are taking the test, I'll read your papers and begin to grade them."

All of the students had brought notebook or laptop computers with them to class as they usually did. They placed the devices on their desks and immediately began typing. The room became quiet except for the light tapping of fingers on keyboards.

Miss Lakely walked around the silent room looking over the students' shoulders. As she did so, she'd glance at sections of their compositions in progress. From time to time she'd walk away to lean forward on the windowsill. She'd stare outside for minutes at a time. Soon the students left the room to retrieve their papers on the network printer.

After they returned to the room, each student handed in their paper to their teacher now seated at her desk.

"Okay, people, I'm going to hand out the test. Of course, we need complete silence during this time. You have until the end of the class period to finish. If there is something you don't understand, please come to me to discuss.

"Now, while you're taking the test, I'll be reading your papers and will comment on them before returning them to you. I will record your grade in my book, but you will not know your final grade until the final class of our session."

Miss Lakely distributed the exam. After the students completed the test they exchanged the exam papers for the composition now marked up with comments. Each then pivoted in silence and left the classroom, eyeing their papers. They each closed the classroom door behind them so as not to interrupt the others still left behind taking the exam.

First, Tyler approached to hand in his test and left the classroom. Amber then followed with Hans not far behind. Becky was next. When she approached Miss Lakely, she stared at the mystery woman who had been at the center of her attention during this summer, and then left the classroom with her composition in hand. She closed the door behind her and then looked at the teacher's comments.

The words were in large print with a fine red-ink marker. They were brief but positive; *"Good job, Becky! You certainly understand the subject matter and how it will apply to your aspiration of becoming a medical research doctor. I wish you luck!"*

She waited out in the hall for Andy, expecting him to be out shortly. After a few minutes with no sign of him, she approached the classroom door and peered through the window.

She couldn't quite see Miss Lakely since Andy's taller body blocked the view. They both seemed to be chuckling as Andy looked intently into his teacher's face and listened closely to every word spoken to him.

Becky couldn't hear the dialogue but could see how they both smiled as they continued chatting. Andy nodded his head several times, seeming to agree with whatever his teacher had told him.

Becky's heart sank as she watched the friendly interaction between the suspicious teacher and her boyfriend. Her mood became sullen before she pivoted and walked away, heading for the main office to begin her part-time job.

After nearly ten minutes of keeping herself busy and chatting with Mrs. Savoyski, she finally saw Andy come into the office. He had a beaming smile as he greeted the two of them sorting and filing near the tall metal cabinets.

"Well, I was wondering if you were ever going to show up for work today, Andy," Becky commented.

She spoke without looking at him, focusing on her stack of manila folders.

"Oh, yeah. Miss Lakely had some things to tell me and we sorta got carried away."

Mrs. Savoyski smiled then excused herself to run out to the Post Office to buy stamps for the office.

"So, you two sorta got carried away, huh?" Becky said, turning to face him and glare into his eyes.

Andy now picked up on the tension in her voice. But without thinking about the consequences, he continued speaking.

"Yeah, kinda, but…but it was good!"

"Good? What the hell does that mean?" Becky's voice didn't veil her emotions.

"Well, just listen to me. Miss Lakely asked me to sit with her for a few minutes and discuss my composition. She really liked it!"

"Oh, she liked your paper but not the rest of ours?"

"No, no, Beck. She was interested in what I had to say about my hopes for a future career in law enforcement. She thinks…"

Becky interrupted him mid-sentence.

"Law Enforcement? What…what are you talking about? You now think you want to be a freakin' cop? Or…or do you want to become some undercover agent breaking up organized crime? You, Andy? When did this pipe dream come into your head? You never mentioned it to me before!"

"Well, I sorta just thought of it during class. I wanted to—you know, make a good impression on Miss Lakely. So my paper was about me wanting to join the FBI. But I don't want to be out into the field as a cop, or an undercover agent. The FBI has huge forensic laboratory network. I would like to work behind the scenes and use my logic and analytical skills to help solve cases. So I wrote about this in my paper and she thought it was well done!"

Becky finished her filing and moved on to tapping data into the computer in front of her.

"Yeah. Geez, that's really good, Andy. I just never thought about lying in my paper. I did something stupid. I wrote about the truth and how I really want to become a medical research doctor."

"Oh, c'mon now. You're all pissed off about something that makes no sense. And besides, I enjoyed having a one on one talk with Miss Lakely. She really is a nice lady. I saw a different side to her and now there is no way I can believe she's involved with some illegal shit. She's just too nice and...and caring. She just doesn't seem like a ruthless criminal. Becky, she talked to me, you know, like a friend. I really felt she was sincere when she told me how she thought I'd make a good FBI analyst."

Becky stared at her taller friend without saying a word. They both let it go and concentrated on their tasks before closing out for the day.

The walk home was quiet, lacking any enthusiasm.

"So, Andy, I take it you don't want to confront Miss Lakely with her involvement in this case as we had planned?"

The lanky young man slowed his gait as they came upon their designated spot to split up and go to their respective homes. As they stopped, they faced one another and he rested his hands gently on Becky's shoulders.

"Look, I know you don't want to hear this, but I was never really into confronting our teacher. I guess I'm just afraid it's a mistake and we'd be making asses of ourselves. Now, I'm more convinced that we are on the wrong trail. I don't think we had her linked into everything correctly, and quite frankly, I'm not interested in going back to the white board with our decision-tree logic. So, I'm just gonna let this whole thing go, Becky. And, I hope you really consider doing the same. Will you do that? Please? It just makes sense to stay out of whatever business isn't our own. We got into this thing so deep, it screwed up our summer vacation. Whatever mystery solving has to be done should be left to the police."

Becky looked up at her friend without any expression. She stared into his eyes then raised her hands to his palms still resting on her shoulders. She gently pulled them off and turned without saying a word, walking solo down the street. Within minutes she was nearing her house, while Andy stood in the same spot, alone and motionless.

CHAPTER NINETEEN

The evening meal at the Bing home was unusually quiet. Becky's parents knew their daughter was bothered by something but they also knew whatever the problem, she'd discuss it with them when and if she wanted to do so.

But before she prepared to leave the table and to bring her emptied plate into the kitchen, Mr. Bing spoke briefly to his daughter to let her know the silence hadn't gone unnoticed.

"Becky, *jin tian wanshang, ni bu jiao tan, mei yu shwo hua. Yu mei yu wenti*? (You've been quiet, not chatting, tonight. Is there a problem?)"

Dr. Bing spoke to her in their native Mandarin. It was a routine they had begun many years ago when she was just a toddler. The pattern was something the family of three enjoyed. During the daylight hours they always spoke English, but from dinnertime onward each evening they'd converse in Mandarin Chinese. It provided an opportunity for Becky to learn Chinese and become bilingual. It was a way for her to connect to her heritage. Mrs. Bing also participated and improved her own Mandarin skills.

"*Mei you wenti, Baba* (there are no problems, Dad)," she responded and asked to be excused from the dinner table.

Upstairs she closed her bedroom door and grabbed her flute out of its hard case. Without consciously thinking about what she was doing, she placed the shiny, chrome instrument up to her lips. She knew the classical tune by heart. It was Prelude to An Afternoon of a Faun, by Claude Debussy. The soft, pastoral music was one of her favorite pieces. The movements were peaceful and mystical. The piece always brought her into a mental and physical balance.

It was Becky's temporary escape from life's challenges. The therapeutic routine helped her separate from the harshness of reality. The soothing chords of music changed her into one of the gossamer mythical characters in Debussy's work. It made her dreamy and light so she could mentally float above things that suddenly seemed unimportant. The soft melody was her drug of choice and it had none of the negative trappings of the alternatives.

Up in the privacy of her bedroom she played her flute for almost an hour before getting ready for a night of reading in bed. Feeling relaxed, she prepared for bed and then took Jane Austen's *Pride and Prejudice* from her bookshelf. The story would block her from reflecting on her fragile relationship with Andy, her enigmatic teacher, and the unspeakable, heinous crimes committed to Cindy Shea and Amber Woods.

As she read the book, she became hooked on the storyline. She turned the pages quickly over the next two hours until her eyes became heavy and she was soon fast asleep.

She awoke in the morning with the sound of the birds chirping outside of her bedroom window. Her digital clock told her it was only five-thirty. Refreshed and energized, she showered and dressed before tip-toeing downstairs so not to awaken her parents.

After gulping down a glass of chilled orange juice and devouring a piece of toast, she jotted a brief note for her parents, leaving it on the kitchen table. Within minutes she was out through the back door and on her bicycle.

But when she cruised down the slight hill to the corner of Bridge Street, she didn't turn south that would lead to North Haven High School. Instead, she turned her handlebars east and headed out toward Hook Island.

While the sun rose in the eastern sky, Becky peddled across the wooden bridge and headed for the off-limits island factories that had presented so many mysteries to her this summer.

She hid her bike then vigilantly looked around to be sure nobody was on the island this early in the morning. Within minutes she had entered the dilapidated structures using the same entrance first used by Miss Lakely, Jack the Biker, and probably the former high school Chemistry teacher, Mr. Barry Jones.

Becky quickly retraced the steps that Andy and she had taken during their last visit to the decrepit textile factory. Within minutes she had reached the dark and dingy vacant office. Nervously, she opened the creaking door, turned on the light switch and stepped over to the desk that had held the lab keys.

With keys in hand, she quietly walked over to the metal door and unlocked it. After reaching inside she flipped on the laboratory light switch.

It was then when her heart stopped.

What she saw before her was not what she had expected. The laboratory was in shambles. The lab workbenches were not orderly as they once had been. They had been moved around and a working stool had been turned over. There were broken beakers and test tubes on the bench and on the cement floor. It looked like someone had ransacked the lab leaving nothing behind intact.

Becky then turned to look for what she had come here on this summer morning to collect. Her eyes panned over to the corner where the cardboard cartons had been stacked holding zip-lock bags with counts of fifty pills each. Now there was nothing there. The corner of the room was cleaned out.

Her mind raced with anger and disappointment. *What the hell went on in here? When did this place get trashed and where the hell did the illegal pills go? Did the cops come in and make a drug bust? But if so, they wouldn't have destroyed all of the chemical laboratory apparatus. This must have just happened recently. It looks like there is no trace of any drug mill here at all.*

Suddenly, a strange sound derailed her train of thought. The creaking sound could only be coming from the inner office door.

There was no time to turn off the light. She'd never make it to the switch. Whoever just came in would quickly see the open laboratory door and the lights turned on inside.

Becky scooted toward the back of the lab. There was just a small space between the wall and a three-tiered scratched and rusted old filing cabinet. She squeezed and lowered her petite body into the tight space.

From where she hid she couldn't see the doorway but could hear the sound of footsteps coming closer to the laboratory. The cadence stopped then continued once again. A shadow now played on the far wall. It was a silhouette that appeared to be a man. The shadow then stopped moving and apparently picked up a piece of the broken glass then dropped it onto the lab workbench with a tingling sound.

Becky's heart pumped uncontrollably as she watched the tall shadow came closer. Her eyes could only look straight ahead. She nervously focused on the underbelly of the lab bench while remaining motionless. Then her eyes zoomed in on what she had come for. Under the far end of the bench was one unopened zip-lock bag of pills. *When the place was destroyed, one bag must have flown under the bench unnoticed*, she thought.

Her eyes then focused on the shadow of the figure now coming closer to her hiding spot behind the file cabinet. The silhouette on the wall was clearer now.

She could see that the person was tall and slender in stature. He appeared to walk slowly as if he was unsure of what he was going to do next. He may have been in awe of what he was seeing or perhaps he was revisiting the scene of what he had destroyed. The man's shadow also showed he had a thick head of hair.

As the figure moved closer to the end of the workbench, her eyes shifted away from the shadow and looked at the lower physical body of the man standing just a few feet away from her. It was then that she noticed the skinny legs and athletic shoes.

I know those skinny legs! I know those athletic shoes!

Despite the risk, Becky gingerly raised her body up so she could take a better glimpse. As soon as she did her eyes opened wider in shock. She couldn't hold back her surprise.

"Andy?"

The tall, slender boy jumped almost a foot into the air with the sudden voice coming from behind him.

"Becky?"

For a moment, the two stood staring at each other.

"What…what the hell are you doing here, Becky? I mean, I thought you'd be in class, and not out here of all places!"

Becky eased her body out of her tight hiding place and faced her friend. "What am I doing here? I thought you gave up on this case. Remember you telling me that we should let it go and leave it all up to the police? You said you didn't want anything more to do with this."

Andy shuffled his feet then answered while avoiding eye contact. "Oh, I don't know. I…I just felt that I let you down. So, I changed my mind and wanted to make it good, maybe even confront Miss Lakely. I even hid a tape recorder into my coronet case as you had suggested. You know, just in case we went ahead and confronted her. But then I figured if I could come back here, I might find some additional evidence that maybe we overlooked. I thought there might be some evidence in the office or here in the lab that would help us solve this case. I sure as hell was surprised to find this place trashed. But what about you, Beck? What the hell are you doing down here this morning?"

"I was thinking along the same lines as you. I hoped there'd be nobody down here at this hour. Even Miss Lakely is teaching our class right now, so she couldn't be here. But I wasn't looking for just any clue. I wanted to get my hands on those pills that we saw last time we were here."

"Yeah, the pills. I noticed all the shipping cartons got cleared out of here. It looked like it was destroyed to leave no trace behind. But...but tell me, why'd you want to get those pills?"

"I wanted to have them evaluated. I'm going to ask my father to see if someone at the School of Medicine can break down the pills and let me know if they are truly the same pills found in Cindy Shea's body. Remember what Tyler told us? It was a combination of three drug rape compounds. I wanted to know if that combination matched the pills made here."

"Ah, too bad. That's a good idea, but now they're all gone," Andy said.

Becky then dropped down to the floor and scooted under the lab bench. She came up holding a zip-lock plastic bag.

"Yeah, but check this out. This one got away. So, I did get what I came for after all!"

"Cool!"

"Now let's get the hell out of here. We can still make it to class just a little late if we spin our butts off!"

"Yeah. But just one more thing, Beck."

She looked up at her friend. "What is it, Andy?"

"Are we still good?"

She raised herself on her tiptoes and gave him a long, moist kiss on his lips.

"Yeah, we're still good," she replied.

Before getting to their bikes a light, misty shower fell softly upon them. Becky pulled out a compact plastic poncho from her saddlebag. She put it on, stretching the hood up over her safety helmet.

Andy grabbed a compact, green umbrella fastened under his bike's cross-bar. He opened the umbrella, displaying a Boston Celtics logo before they spun off to the high school.

CHAPTER TWENTY

With the misty drizzle letting up, Becky and Andy locked up their ten-speeds to the bike rack. Becky peeled of her poncho.

"You know, Andy, I think we're running out of time. That drug mill on Hook Island doesn't exist anymore. Those cartons of pills we had seen are now all out of there. The equipment was either gone or trashed. I'm thinking we might be too late. Even if I get these pills evaluated, the bad guys, whoever they are, will be long gone. What do you think?"

Andy nodded his head in agreement.

"Yeah, I was thinking about that while we biked here. Now there's no real evidence of any illegal operation going on there. The only people we actually saw connected to that crap were 'Jack the Biker' and Miss Lakely. And, we know that Jack is dead."

"Miss Lakely is the only one who knows more about what went on down there than you and me. I'm thinking we'd better go back to Plan A. So, I'm bringing in my coronet case with the mini-tape recorder inside. But…but are you up for this?"

Becky looked over at her grinning friend.

"Up for it? Am I up for it? It was my freakin' idea, you wise ass!" she said.

The two spent some time going over the steps of their plan. When they were satisfied they had it worked out they stepped up the school staircase. Andy carried his umbrella in one hand, his coronet case in the other.

Everyone in the classroom watched in silence as the dampened couple arrived late to class. There were smirks and smiles from students and teacher alike who knew Becky was now dating Andy.

No words were spoken as they quietly took their seats. Miss Lakely continued with her discussion, telling the students she wouldn't ask them to read their career composition to their peers, but opted to summarize each paper without disclosing who had written it. After doing so, she told the teens their final test and course grades would be distributed the following morning, the last day of summer school.

* * *

The summer AP Logic class ended and soon Amber, Tyler, and Hans hustled through the door. But Becky and Andy dawdled behind waiting to be alone in the classroom with Miss Lakely. This was the first step in their plan to confront their teacher.

Andy busied himself closing and clasping his large, green umbrella with the Boston Celtics basketball logo. After a long minute, Becky approached the teacher still sitting at her desk, busy jotting down notes in her grade book.

"Excuse me, Miss Lakely, I...ah...I mean we, Andy and I, have a few questions to ask you if you have a few minutes."

"Oh, sure, I'm not looking forward to leaving to go out in such dismal and dreary weather. It's really not a beach day today, eh guys?"

Becky desperately tried to hide her nervousness. She knew Andy would remain quiet during these first tense moments.

"If you don't mind, we need to show you something but...but it's not here with us right now. It's ah, something we discovered upstairs in the reference library, and we need your opinion about it. Can you please spend a few minutes while we show it to you?"

Amanda Lakely's brow furled at the unexpected request. She looked up at Becky quizzically and then over to an obviously nervous Andy Abbot.

"Well, I can't imagine what you want to show me, but ah…okay, sure. I'll walk with you guys upstairs to the library."

Andy's eyes followed his teacher's every move while she turned to pick up her large, straw handbag sitting on the floor. She put her grade book into the bag, clasped it, and stood up to leave.

The two teens stared at the shoulder bag, wondering if the handgun was inside. They both were convinced it was. Suddenly, Andy stopped at the base of the stairs. He was performing his act just as Becky and he had verbally rehearsed outside of the building before class.

"Oh, I just remembered. I left my coronet case back in the room and I gotta leave right from here for my lesson. I'll catch up with you two in a few minutes."

Miss Lakely and Becky continued up the stairs.

Andy jogged back to the classroom and picked up his coronet case from the classroom floor. Again, as planned with Becky, he opened up the hard case and turned on his mini-tape recorder inside. He checked to see that the thin, black microphone was duct-taped to the small air flow vent in the case. Confident that everything was in place, he closed the instrument case and left the classroom. Soon he was galloping up the stairs to catch up with his teacher and best friend.

There were a few students scattered around in the large reference room despite the summer month. Some were working part-time for the summer, labeling books and discarding older editions. The librarian smiled at them as they walked by her desk.

Becky was relieved there were some students sitting at the computer corrals. The summer-help students pushed cartloads of books and periodical magazines.

The three of them took seats at a long, oak reading table at the furthest corner of the library. Miss Lakely sat on one side; the two students sat across from her.

Becky cleared her throat then began, trying to present a confident composure. Her eyes stayed fixed on her teacher as she spoke.

"First of all, Miss Lakely, I want to thank you for meeting with us," she said, speaking in a near whisper.

"Sure, of course, kids. But what did you want to show me up here in the library? Is it something to do with a philosopher you came across in your research?"

Becky swallowed hard while contemplating her pre-planned script.

"Oh, I'll get to that in a minute. First, let me tell you what Andy and I have discovered in the past few weeks and…but it isn't about the class research and it's not about any philosopher. It concerns you, Miss Lakely."

The teacher's eyebrows suddenly arched with curious anticipation. "Oh?"

"You first have to understand what we discovered not only had to do with you, but with…with others connected to North Haven High School."

"Becky, please get to your point," Amanda Lakely said, now appearing to lose patience.

Arming herself with a deep breath, Becky continued speaking. But before she could get her next words out, Andy interrupted her.

"Miss Lakely, we, Becky and I, have been out to Hook Island. We managed to go underground and on a couple of occasions we saw you there."

Amanda Lakely's complexion quickly turned to a soft pink. The reaction was so uncharacteristic of the teacher who always seemed in control. It was clear she wasn't expecting such a revelation while sitting at the school library table. Before she could say anything, Andy continued with a strong and confident conviction in his voice.

"We also saw you talk to the same man who was found shot to death and pulled out of Peck's Pond.

But…but you never came forward to identify that man to the police. According to the local police report, the FBI identified him as some drug-dealing ring leader."

Miss Lakely now leaned back slightly in her chair. Andy leaned in closer to her from across the table so he could still speak in a soft whispering tone.

"Becky and I later returned to that underground office. We discovered it's connected to a chemical laboratory of some kind. That lab there manufactures pills, illegal pills. And, we think those pills are date-rape drugs."

"Oh?"

"And we're having them tested right now as we speak," Andy lied.

The teacher's eyes now widened. It was clear she was shocked at what she was hearing. Now it was Becky's time to speak to the teacher.

"We have more to tell you, but right now we want to hear from you, Miss Lakely. And if you don't give us some answers, we're calling the police right after we leave here and tell them about our findings."

Amanda Lakely's complexion now faded from the hot pink to a whiter shade of pale. She had absorbed what she heard from the two sixteen year-olds. It was obvious she was taken off guard hearing about their recent discoveries. She now appeared to be at a loss for words.

"Listen, kids, I…I can explain," she said in a whisper, panning around the library to ensure nobody was within earshot. But then the teacher's hand quickly reached out to grab her straw bag sitting on the table. With one sweeping motion, she slid it toward her and unclasped the opening.

Becky's eyes widened. Her heart suddenly dropped into her stomach as she expected the gun to be pulled out from the bag. Her plan wasn't going to work despite there being other people nearby.

WHAAAAAAP!

The sudden noise exploded, startling everyone inside the high-ceiling reference room. All eyes turned to the corner reading table.

The frightening explosive sound had come from Andy's Boston Celtics umbrella. He had whipped it down on top of the straw handbag and the wooden table. It had just barely missed crushing Amanda Lakely's hand.

"What...what the fuck are you doing? You just scared the crap out of me!" Miss Lakely angrily whispered after pulling her hand back down under the table.

The other students and librarian watched, and then politely turned back to what they were doing.

"What the hell were you just reaching for inside of your bag? Your gun?" Andy replied angrily in a low whisper. "We also know about the weapon you carry inside your handbag. Is that the same gun that killed the man who was dumped into Peck's Pond?"

The teacher now leaned inward, resting her elbows on the table. Her shaking hand now massaged her forehead as if she suddenly had a painful migraine headache.

"My God!" Miss Lakely finally said with a sigh. "You two have done your little investigation, haven't you?"

"You got that right," Andy replied.

The two gave each other icy stares for a moment.

"Andy, I was just reaching for my wallet inside my bag. Here, you guys open it up and take out my wallet."

She slid the handbag back across the table toward Becky, who cautiously slipped her hand inside while keeping an eye riveted on her teacher. Her fingers soon felt the cold steel of the concealed handgun. Then her hand felt the soft leather form of a wallet. She pulled it out of the straw bag. The oversized navy-blue wallet was snapped closed. She briefly looked at it then slid it over to her teacher.

"No, no. You open it if it will make you two feel better," she said sliding back over to her student.

Becky unclasped the wallet.

"Now look for my driver's license inside the detachable leather holder," Miss Lakely instructed, still in a soft whisper. It was evident she now had something of her own to show the young super-sleuths.

Becky found the laminated document. She stared at the State of Connecticut-issued photo-ID driver's license. She likewise responded in a library-correct whisper.

"So what? This only tells us that you're Amanda Lakely." She looked down again at the license. "And, you're five-foot-six and weigh one hundred and thirty pounds. And you live on Sheppard Avenue in Hamden, Connecticut. This doesn't mean a freakin' thing!"

"I know, I know. But now look inside that leather license holder once again. There's a hidden compartment closed tight with a tiny Velcro strip. It's designed to look like it is part of the wallet. Open that up and see what's inside."

Becky fingered open the secret slit and once again pulled out another laminated ID card. Andy leaned close to her so he could read the small card. This laminated identification had another, older, photo of their teacher. But the name under the mug shot wasn't Amanda Lakely. It was Amanda White. And, the ID wasn't just another driver's license. There was an official government seal holograph on it with the words—Federal Bureau of Investigation, Drug Enforcement Agency.

Becky showed the ID to Andy.

"Oh my God! You're...you're...you're an FBI agent!" Andy gasped. "You work for the DEA. You're not really a teacher; you're a law enforcement officer!"

Amanda now looked around and whispered her response.

"That's right, guys, I am not a teacher. But what I want you to know is that I am not a criminal. I catch criminals. Now, there's a phone number to a federal office on that ID card. You can call it to verify who I am. That's what it's there for."

A silent pause now hung in the rear corner of the library until Andy asked his next question.

"But...but what are you doing? I mean, we thought...."

Amanda held up her hand in the universal "stop" signal. She continued to keep her voice just above a whisper.

"Look, since you two already stumbled across some sensitive information, I have to let you in on the case we're working on." She looked around once again to ensure nobody was within earshot.

The two teens leaned closer across the table toward their teacher.

"We've been working on this illegal drug mill case for a while. I was assigned to it in November and we arranged to get me hired as the replacement teacher to Mr. Jones. But you two already know that."

Andy's head turned to Becky at the mention of the former teacher's name. Agent Amanda White continued her story.

"This is a very complex case. I'm an undercover operative working as a teacher at North Haven High. My partner is another undercover cop working as a North Haven Police officer."

"An undercover cop in our police force? What the hell is that all about?" Becky asked.

"I'll get to that in a bit. Last fall, we discovered that Mr. Pratt had partnered with someone to create the drug lab out at Hook Island. So, when I interviewed with him for the teaching job, I told him I was a good teacher, but had only worked in a "substitute" capacity and needed a break to start my career. I then purposely confided in him that I had a very secret and checkered past, selling drugs during my college days. I lied, telling him I ended up with a minor conviction. I pleaded for him to take me on for just one year, since I needed to get experience. If he did, I would resign then return to my home state of Indiana for a permanent career."

"Oh my God...is that true?" Andy asked, now startled at such a revelation.

"No, no, of course not! She grinned at the question. "But just to let you two know, the agency provides us with professional acting lessons during our undercover training. And, we're also trained on how to hook in unsuspecting drug leaders. Our intelligence network suspected Pratt was in the drug mill business for a quick buck and only a short term. He wanted to make his money unloading the date-rape drugs to another distributer as soon as possible. He'd retire with a large sum of money and be gone by the end of this summer."

"Hmm. So, that's why he just announced his early retirement!" Andy commented.

"That's right. He's right on schedule according to our 'intel' that we get passed down to us."

"But how did you get to work for Pratt inside the underground drug mill?" Becky asked.

"After we had our confidential interview, it was his turn to confide in me. Then he made me a deal. He'd give me the teaching job if I worked for him part-time in his ah...extra-curricular operation. He wanted me to do just some clerical work packaging and counting bags of pills and stuff like that. And that's exactly what I needed to get closer so we could break this case. Most times I was with somebody else inside the lab. That's when I met Jones, who ran the drug lab's chemical operation making the drug-rape pills."

"So where does 'Jack the biker' come in?" Becky asked.

Amanda chuckled at Becky's reference.

"Jack was a CI who was assigned to work on this case. Do you guys know what a CI is?"

Both of the teenagers shook their heads in the negative.

"Well, CI stands for Confidential Informant. These people are used by cops all over the country. Jack was an ex-con who wanted to go straight, so the agency helped him if he'd help us out. Typically, a CI goes underground for the cops and mixes in with the criminals, a lot like an undercover agent. Then he secretly reports back to the agency. Jack had been working for the FBI for several years back out in Chicago. He had actually worked on a lot of drug cases in many different states. His reputation made him perfect to be assigned to this case shortly after I got hired. He had no car when he arrived and Jones let him use his motorcycle most of the time. So, you see that wasn't Jack's bike, it belongs to Jones."

"Hmm. And now he's...he's dead, murdered," Andy added.

"Yes. And that was so unfortunate. Jack was getting over-anxious to close this case. Part of it was he felt badly that some of the drugs may have already been released locally apart from the major deal. From what we learned, Pratt never wanted the drug distributed in this area. He had buyers from LA who would buy the whole lot from him. When we learned that forensics found Cindy Shea had date rape drugs in her system, we didn't know if her death was connected to this case or not. We still are not totally sure, because we don't have enough evidence. And as you both know, when Tyler Farnham spoke during our class, it made me react as well. But we still have no real evidence and that's something we're working on."

"So, you had just met Jack, or whoever he really is, recently?" Becky asked.

"Yeah, and that *is* his real name, not the name of Richard Baker that the agency gave to the local police for media purposes. But I think Jack must have tripped up some way or he was 'made' through some other source. Evidently Pratt found out about him or perhaps Pratt's nephew got some information on him previously working with the FBI."

"Nephew? Who...who the hell is Pratt's nephew?" Andy asked.

"Oh, well, that's our agency's investigation currently underway with the North Haven Police. I thought maybe you knew that Pratt's nephew, Nate Simpson, is a local cop and is a 'bad' cop. He's not out in the field but works in the Communications Unit. He's only a dispatcher type of cop. We had intelligence telling us he intercepts a lot of confidential information and ruins criminal sting operations for his own payback. So, before I came here we arranged to get our own undercover cop assigned into NHPD. He's supposed to be a transfer rookie but he's really here to get a closer look at Officer Simpson."

"So that's why there were no further charges or publicity after that raid on Hook Island. This cop, Nate Simpson, had it squashed."

"That's right, but that's only part of it! And now, you can appreciate how happy I am you confronted me today instead of going straight to the cops. God only knows what Simpson would do if you reported to him what you have uncovered."

"God, this is so freakin' weird!" Andy commented.

"So, the local police can never know what I'm doing or anything about me. Otherwise, the whole case will be blown. Now, can I count on you guys to keep this secret? You can never contact the police until after this case is closed!"

A long pause hung in the air. Becky turned to Andy who was looking into her eyes for a reaction.

"But...but who killed Jack the...the CI?" Becky asked. "Was it Mr. Pratt?"

"We're not sure at this point. But once we move in and get an arrest on the entire drug production, we feel the 'perps' will talk."

"Why can't you just arrest Pratt now?"

"We're still missing some final pieces to the puzzle. As soon as we get those, we'll get the word from our higher-ups to make our move." Agent Amanda White paused for a moment. "Now I have to trust you two will not divulge anything we discussed here today. You cannot, and I emphasize *cannot* inform the North Haven Police Department."

An awkward pause hung once again in the air. It was obvious the whole case now rested on whether or not they trusted their teacher. And that decision to trust her or not had to be made right now. In a minute or so she'd leave the library. She could have just duped them if the FBI identification card was a phony. Then she'd escape. The pseudo teacher would never be seen again and the case would never be solved.

Becky thought how she played her chess game strategy well and cornered the teacher in a public place for the confrontation. But her skeptic mind wouldn't rest. And the last move had yet to be executed.

Maybe she is an FBI agent. But her emphasizing that we cannot contact the local cops is something I really can't feel comfortable with. It sounds like it's a ploy and gives her time to get out of the state, assume a new identity. I can certainly verify that quickly after we break up, but it will be too late then. Checkmate. The pretty, young teacher/killer wins the game.

. "I really need you not to contact the police or tell anyone about this until the case is completely solved. If you let this out or contact the police—the case is gone forever. Now, you guys do want to help the FBI, don't you?"

"Of course, Miss Lakely. Ah, we should still call you, Miss Lakely, right?" Andy asked.

"Yeah, I need you to continue using my cover name."

"Ah, we…umm, Andy and I, have some things we now want to tell you, especially since we now know who you really are."

The young, attractive woman jerked her head back in dramatic fashion. But her serious expression remained.

"Aha, so you have more surprises to tell me in addition to spying on me out at Hook Island?"

Becky then told her about Amber Woods' experience out at Bantam Lake. She further explained how Mr. Pratt had lured her out to his cabin during the April school vacation. As she disclosed the sordid date-rape account, she mentally dismissed her promise to Amber to never tell anyone of the sick sexual attack.

"Does Amber suspect that Mr. Pratt raped her?" Amanda asked.

Becky then explained the difficult situation with Amber's horrible experience.

"She doesn't think it was him. But she told Andy and me that she kept seeing images of some bizarre, weird guy her dreams. It may have been hallucinations from the drugs. She told us she couldn't identify him."

"That's the new drug formula all right! It relaxes and confuses its victims and then causes a form of amnesia with minor hallucinations," Amanda said.

"But she told us she also heard the sound of a motorcycle. Do you think that...that your CI, this ah, ex-con Jack, could have raped Amber after she was drugged up at Bantam Lake?"

The acting high school teacher leaned forward once again in her chair. Her eyes glazed over for a moment in deep thought before she responded.

"To be honest with you, I don't know for sure. Of course, Jack wasn't an FBI agent, only a hired and paid informant. I really didn't know him that well. Part of his assignment was to call upon Pratt, to become a fake drug distributor and negotiator to sell the date-rape pills for the highest bid. Of course, he never sold on the street. He always stalled the financial deals, giving us more time to pull everything together. There was a lot of money to be made, but Pratt needed a 'dirt man' and Jack could certainly do that."

"Geez, just how much money is involved for Pratt to take all these risks?" Andy asked.

"When I started working for Pratt inside the factory, I estimated the street value of this newly created pill inventory to be over ten million dollars. Pratt and his drug-chemist, ah...your former homeroom teacher, Barry Jones, would walk away with nearly half of that amount after the deal was made."

"I still can't believe Jack wasn't the creepy guy who raped Amber. He looked like that angry, screwed-up type. You know what I mean. He had the long hair and his arms were covered in tattoos," Andy said.

"Yeah, well, that helped with his cover for the agency. But I hope he wouldn't have any part of a sexual attack on a teenager, especially during this case. Perhaps he rode the bike up to the cabin to meet with Pratt and then left. It's the only place Pratt would meet with Jack. You can understand why. Your principal could never be seen publicly with a tattooed biker. You know, I'm thinking Amber may have heard him pull away on his motorcycle as she was coming to. And if she had been asleep in the bedroom as you told me, Jack wouldn't have known she was hidden inside the cabin. If this happened back in April, I know he would have reported that to me."

"So what happens next? I mean this crap can't go on for much longer. We all know Pratt is retiring and moving on. And he's guilty! He'll probably take off for Europe or some other country real soon."

"Right, Becky. And my job is to keep a close eye on your principal and report anything unusual in the next forty-eight hours. But now that Jack is out of the picture, it became Barry Jones's job to finish off the drug deal with the LA people. But we just learned that Pratt's nephew, Officer Nate Simpson, is trying to get a commission by finding his own buyer. So things are up in the air, but moving fast. Even though Simpson is a behind the scenes guy, he stands to make a lot of money out of this deal, too!"

"Geez, this is more freakin' complicated than I ever imagined!" Becky said.

"You know, with what you just told me about Amber Woods, and the nagging questions about the Cindy Shea fatality, I think you just put the final nail in the coffin. I'm calling my boss to see if we can make our move right away. And if...."

Suddenly, Agent Amanda White stopped talking. Her eyes looked up and over the heads of the two students sitting at the reading table.

A man's heavy footsteps were approaching.

"Oh, Mr. Pratt! Ah...Becky and Andy asked for some help on their summer school research project. I'm sorry if I kept them from their job in the office. We were just finishing up. "

"Oh, that's quite all right, Amanda."

The students turned to look up at the administrator with his usual cunning grin on his face. His nickname so aptly fit when the silver-haired man smiled.

They both stood up, preparing to leave the library.

"Oh, sit down kids, sit down. I just need to speak with your teacher for a moment privately out in the hallway. I just have a couple of questions I need to ask Miss Lakely. She'll ah...she'll be right back. Oh, and I wanted to tell you kids that Mrs. Savoyski won't need your assistance today. She already left for the day."

Pratt quietly escorted Amanda out of the library into the hallway as Becky and Andy remained sitting at the reading table. Andy turned to Becky with a relaxed expression.

"Let's wait 'til she returns for her handbag before we get the hell out of here. I don't like this, do you? I mean we know that Pratt is a freakin' criminal and now the two of them are together. I mean, I want to trust what Miss Lakely just told us, but if...if she was lying to us and her FBI card is a phony...we...."

"Yeah, I know what you're thinking," Becky said with some nervousness in her voice. "She'd better come back soon. And they're putting out the lights in the library here. It'll be closed soon."

"Well, I'm going to believe her. We really don't have a choice and if you think about it, Miss Lakely, I mean, Amanda White, was the missing piece to our mystery puzzle. It does all makes sense now, her being an undercover agent and all that. With her bird-dogging Pratt and his asshole partner, Jones, I bet she arrests them real soon."

"Yeah. Although I was a little surprised to hear that Jack the Biker was also working for the FBI," Becky responded. "But we still don't know who shot him or why."

"Oh, Beck. C'mon for God's sake. It's over! Let's leave everything up to the pros."

They were next interrupted by the middle-aged librarian who approached them at the table.

"I'm sorry kids, but we're closing for today. We'll be open at nine tomorrow morning if you still have more work to do here," she said with a smile.

Andy stood up, picked up his folded umbrella and coronet case and turned to leave.

"Oh, ah wait a minute, Andy...I'll just take this," Becky said, reaching out to grab Miss Lakely's straw handbag. The two of them ambled out of the library and into the darkened, tiled corridor. But when they looked around there was no sign of their teacher or Principal, Alfonse Pratt.

The hallway was in complete darkness.

CHAPTER TWENTY-ONE

The darkened hallway seemed eerie with the solemn quiet that now filled it. As the duo walked briskly down the long, tiled corridor, they peered into every doorway to look for their teacher and principal.

"Where the hell did they go?" Andy asked, no longer whispering. "I thought the 'ol' silver fox' was only going to be a minute with Amanda. Do you think they went downstairs to his office to talk?"

Without another word, they quickly trotted down the staircase, their footsteps echoing inside the stone cinder-block stairwell. There were no lights on at the first level. They quickly paced down to the main office suite. They expected to see lights on as they peered in the window. But there were none. The entire area was in darkness.

"Hey, let's see if Mr. Pratt's car is still in his reserved parking space," Andy said, walking briskly towards the windows facing the back of the building where the faculty parking lot was located.

But Mr. Pratt's Volvo was gone.

"He must have taken off, Becky. But Miss Lakely's car is still here."

"Yeah, and it looks like he took our beloved teacher with him."

"Beck, do you think he took her up to his cabin at Bantam Lake?"

"Yep, I do."

"Oh, my God! Now we...we gotta call the police. We have no choice. Do you think she told Pratt about us and...and what we know?"

"No. I think he found out about Miss Lakely. I think he now knows she, like Jack, was an undercover agent working on this case. Andy, she could be in real danger. This is just too freakin' weird!" she cried out, her voice echoing in the emptied hall.

His face washed with relief when Becky pulled her cell phone out of her blue cotton shorts. She quickly tapped in a few numbers.

"Thank God! You're finally calling 911," he said. "Let's have the cops finish this thing off!"

Becky turned away to speak into her BlackBerry.

"Hello, Amber? Hi, this is Becky Bing! Ah...I'm fine. But listen, Andy and I need your help as quickly as possible. It's an emergency! Can you drive to the back of the high school right away?"

There was a pause.

"Oh, you're driving near here now? Good. I'll explain everything when you get here."

Andy looked at his friend and let out an audible sigh in disbelief of what he just heard.

"Let's go! Hurry! Amber will be here within five minutes," Becky said, leading the way.

They jogged out of the school building and onto the designated rear parking lot. The ground was still damp from the morning rain, but the dark clouds now gave way to a humid sunshine.

Andy held his folded umbrella in hand, while Becky clutched onto their teacher's straw handbag. Their eyes panned around the rear of the school grounds and lot.

There was nobody in sight.

"Becky, what the hell are you doing? Why are you bringing Amber into this? She has enough problems to deal with without us bringing her into our freakin' murder mystery case."

"Listen, for now, we can't call the cops. Weren't you listening upstairs in the library? We'd blow this whole case that the FBI has been working on. And Amber is a key person now, just like Miss Lakely was before we met with her up in the library. And right now, we need Amber."

"Huh? Why the hell do we need Amber now?"

"Because she can take us to the cabin up at Bantam Lake."

"Oh, no…oh, no. I can't do this, Becky. Look, I'm really not as courageous as you might think. My bravery has been tested many times this summer and I was up to the task. But…but now I'm drawing a line on this thing."

Becky paused and looked at him, trying not to chuckle aloud. She stared at him, quietly digesting what he just told her.

"Bravery? Are you talking about your…your bravery?"

Before he could answer, the SUV drove up to meet them. The attractive blonde sat behind the steering wheel. Her hair was pulled back with a headband. She had a puzzled expression on her face. Becky quickly approached the driver's window.

"Amber, listen, we really need your help! We think Mr. Pratt has taken or kidnapped Miss Lakely. And we're pretty sure he's taken her up to his cabin at Bantam Lake. We're worried and don't know what he's going to do to her."

"But…why don't you just call the police?"

"It's complicated and I can explain all of it once we get driving. The question is do you think you can remember how to get to Pratt's cabin up at the lake?"

"Huh? Oh, sure! I was completely alert on the drive up there. I know exactly how to get to his cabin. Hey, you guys jump in. I'll take you up there!"

"Cool!"

Becky grabbed Andy's hand and pulled him with her to the opposite side of the vehicle. She opened his door first and nearly forced him into the back seat. After the two belted themselves in, Becky began telling the story. She told Amber what they had just learned about Miss Lakely and her role as an FBI undercover agent. She further disclosed what they had discovered about the date-rape drug business of which Mr. Pratt was the ring leader.

"I can't believe it! But how…how the hell did you two uncover all this stuff? I mean this is really bizarre!"

As the SUV sped northward along Interstate Route 91, Becky and Andy told Amber the story about Hook Island, Jack the Biker, and Mr. Pratt.

Amber was flabbergasted at what she was hearing from her two new friends.

"I…I just can't believe our sick 'eff-ing' principal is connected with a major drug ring. And, with his position, I can't believe he set this all up by himself. He…he seems so freakin' needy and unable to do anything without help from others. That's…that's why I went up to his cabin in the first place. He needed help with his computer and he offered to pay me to fix it."

"Well, Amber, we know he also has a partner. Do you remember the Science teacher who only lasted a few months at the beginning of the school year? His name is Mr. Jones, Barry Jones."

"Uh, no…but the name is familiar. I didn't take any science courses this year or last. I think I may have heard about him in the fall, but I really never saw him," Amber responded, driving just above the speed limit.

"Well, anyway, he's the chemist who manufactures the drugs for the underground operation. Pratt put up the money for the Hook Island lab, and he had those nasty pills manufactured out there."

"So how long does it take to get up to Pratt's cabin, Amber?" Andy asked.

"Ah…I guess about thirty to forty minutes. We'll be near the exit for Torrington soon."

Amber drove quietly for several minutes. All three of them were silent as they fell into deep thought. Soon,

Amber took the exit for Torrington and points toward Bantam Lake.

Becky guessed what her friend was thinking as she steered toward the location of her sexual attack. It was evident by the single teardrop meandering down her face. After a few miles on a country road lined with leafy maple and elm trees, they came upon a sign with an arrow pointed toward Bantam Lake. The SUV took a sharp left turn onto a dirt road.

"Amber, I think we should be really careful now. If you can, pull off somewhere not too close to Pratt's cabin."

"Okay," she replied, slowing the vehicle over the bumpy road. "I know his place is just a little way down this road. I think all of these short roads lead right to the lake."

"Why not pull over here? We can walk through the woods to get to his place." Becky said.

The blonde senior responded, slowly turning into a small opening along the muddy road. She put on the brakes and turned off the engine.

"Okay, guys, we're here. I remember Pratt's cabin is right on the lake. If you look through the trees you can see the roof from here."

"Okay, Becky, so what's your plan from here?" Andy asked with a twinge of nervousness in his voice.

All three of them looked through the dense trees and wild brush, while Becky responded.

"I want Amber to stay here in the car. Andy, you and I can sneak through the woods to see if Miss Lakely is inside the cabin. From here we can't see any cars outside. But if we spot Mr. Pratt's Volvo, maybe we can sneak up to the cabin and take a peek inside."

An audible gulp came from Andy's throat.

"No, no I want to go with you, Becky. If I can help you guys, I want to be close by," Amber said.

The three slid out of the car with Becky leading the way, still clutching Miss Lakely's straw handbag. They brushed aside low leafy branches as they marched toward the isolated cabin.

Within minutes, they could see the southern side of the lakeside home as they stepped closer to their target. Mr. Pratt's Volvo SUV was parked at the rear of the building. The rear hatch door was left open. Several cardboard cartons stacked inside the vehicle could be seen from their vantage point. But then Becky spotted something that made her suddenly stop in her footsteps.

A Yamaha motorcycle was parked near the front entrance. It was the same bike that Jack, the confidential informant, had ridden before his murder.

Suddenly the front door to the cabin opened. Out walked Mr. Barry Jones. His platinum blonde hair stood out against the background of the dark earth colors. The gold chain around his neck shined once again in the hazy sunlight. He walked past his Yamaha bike and toward the Volvo SUV. Amber grabbed Becky's wrist and held it painfully tight.

"Oh...oh, my God. That's him! That's him!" Amber said with a pained voice.

"Who?" Andy whispered.

"He's the creep who I keep seeing over and over in my nightmares. I think he's...he's the creep who raped me!" She blurted a sob, but not loud enough to bring attention to them standing in the woods.

Their eyes all focused on Barry Jones. The strange man opened the hatch door to the vehicle. He next lifted out a cardboard carton and carried it into the house.

Becky recognized the cardboard carton. It was one of those same containers she had discovered in the underground lab. Each had been stuffed with plastic bags filled with date-rape pills.

Jones soon returned and continued the routine, transferring all of the cartons out of Pratt's car and into the cabin.

Becky spoke in a whisper. "Okay, now we have to act fast! Amber, I want you to stay right here. Listen, I need you to dial 911 when I give you the signal Ah

....let's see. I'll have Miss Lakely's shoulder bag with me. When you see me shift it from one shoulder to the other, make the call."

"Okay, I'll keep an eye out for your signal," she replied, now regaining some composure.

"Hey Andy, here's the plan. You and I can sneak around the back of the house through the woods here so we can't be seen. Once we get there, I want to get close to the cabin and peek inside the windows to see if we can spot Miss Lakely. I just hope she's all right. Then, Amber, look for my signal soon after that."

Andy quickly raised a concern.

"Wait a minute, Beck. If we call the police it might get intercepted according to what Lakely told us. That cop, you know, Pratt's nephew, Nate Simpson, might find out. So, shouldn't we call the FBI directly?"

"Don't worry. Amber's 911 cell phone call will go to the *local* police. We're not in North Haven anymore. Only the town cops here will respond to the emergency and come." Andy knew he should have thought of that before he raised his issue.

The two quickly left Amber alone in the lush woods. They scooted through the wild vegetation, crouching down. Running in short sprints, they stopped behind trunks of the leafy trees. Within minutes they were at the rear side of the lakeside cabin, hunkered down in the thick, green brush. Andy looked over to Becky.

"Look, we have to make a decision right now! We can get ourselves killed in the next five minutes. What if someone sees us running around back here? We know that they already shot and killed our tattooed biker-informant. If they catch us, we'll be their next victims. C'mon, Becky, take out your phone now and call the freakin' cops."

"Look, we came here to do something. Let's finish the job!"

Andy's voice now weakened as he whispered among the wild shrubs. "I told you earlier. I'm not some macho hero you want me to be. This shit is way above us and has been since the summer began. This sneak attack on the cabin just doesn't make any freakin' sense. I…I don't think I can do this, Becky. I'm…I'm really scared."

Becky looked into the nervous blue eyes. Beads of sweat now dotted his pale forehead. His face twitched with fear and perhaps some embarrassment from his honest confession.

She reached over, still with her eyes locked on his, and gently took his hand. Without speaking, she caressed his palm with her fingers and massaged his hand and wrist. The gentle touch brought a smile to his face. His twitching stopped and his smile widened. She was telling him with her gentle massage—we can do this!

"We're going to be all right, Andy. You just have to trust me. Okay, let's go, now, right now!" she said, yanking him up and running toward the cabin's backyard still hand in hand.

With no apparent activity outside of the cabin, Becky and Andy sprinted toward a window on the backside of the vacation home. Crouching low on either side of the window, they waited, catching their breath before Becky carefully stood up peek inside.

Without a word, Becky pointed and waved Andy to stand up and look inside at the bedroom. They both stood to the side of the window, looking through a sheer bedroom curtain. Their mouths dropped open at what they saw.

Lying on the top of the queen-sized bed was their teacher, Miss Lakely. She was motionless on top of the bedspread appearing as though she was in a deep sleep.

Suddenly, another person appeared, stepping inside the bedroom. He closed the door behind him. They could easily identify the man as Mr. Barry Jones.

He leaned over the still woman then sat on the bed, shaking her body slightly to awaken her. He bent down to speak something into her ear. But his voice was too low for the teens to make out what he said.

As she lay there, Miss Lakely nodded her head slowly to answer Jones's question. It was apparent she was heavily drugged and she looked as though she didn't understand where she was or who was with her in the bedroom. She slowly sat up on the side of the bed to face the perverted misfit. Then she smiled as the criminal sex offender once again said something to her. But the words were spoken softly, inaudible to the two stalkers peering through the window.

But when the two teens watched as their teacher unbuttoned her blouse, they immediately turned to stare at one another.

Andy's face twisted into an intense and angry expression. But it also spoke of a new level of courage and determination that immediately overcame him.

"Let's get inside there right away!" Andy whispered incensed at the crime about to take place.

Becky and Andy crouched down and scooted around to the front of the cabin. She kept his hand in hers keeping him in tow. They quietly snuck up onto the front of the contemporary-styled farmer's porch.

She pivoted then looked out across the densely overgrown woods. She spotted Amber's blonde hair in the sea of green thicket. Slowly she transferred the straw shoulder bag from one shoulder to the other to signal to Amber to make the 911 call. She then turned and knocked loudly on the front door.

Within a few seconds the door opened.

A shocked Mr. Pratt greeted them. The two students marched into the house, forcing their principal to backpedal into the foyer.

"Ah…but…but…Becky, Andy…what…what the hell are you two doing here?"

Becky answered his question.

"We're here to give you a choice, Mr. Pratt. First go into that bedroom and tell Mr. Jones to stop what he's doing. And you, you can sit over there in that chair until the cops come."

"What…what the hell are you talking about? Cops, what cops?"

Without a word, Becky quickly reached into Miss Lakely's handbag and pulled out her thirty-eight caliber handgun.

She pointed the barrel of the weapon directly at her principal's head.

"Get Jones out of that bedroom, right now!" she yelled. Pratt looked at the shiny barrel of the gun aimed directly at his forehead. He kept his eyes riveted on Becky's hand, tightly gripping the heavy steel weapon as she followed steps behind him.

"Now listen, Becky! Just lower that gun now, and give it to me. We can discuss all of this. There is a total misunderstanding here." Pratt spoke loudly so that his partner, Barry Jones, could hear him.

As Becky cocked the trigger of the gun, Andy stepped over to the fireplace. He grabbed the black, iron poker from its stand. Holding it tightly, he returned to stand beside Becky.

The sleazy Barry Jones now came out of the bedroom and walked down the hallway leading to the foyer. Becky played the gun back and forth from one man to the other.

"Now, listen, young lady, we can straighten this out for you right now," Jones said, stepping towards her in an intimidating manner.

He never stopped walking towards her. When he came within a couple of feet of the petite Becky, he quickly lunged out, attempting to grab the gun from her grip.

Becky, nervous and stunned, let the weapon fall from her hands and onto the knotty pine, plank floor. But she recovered quickly from her frozen state and leapt for the gun before Mr. Jones could get to it.

Jones tried to snatch up the weapon.

But Andy stomped on Jones's hand just as he tried to grab at it. Still with his foot and his total body weight on the man's hand, he reached down to pick up the gun.

Jones yelled out then wrestled himself free. He stood up ready to attack the taller boy.

But the young student dropped the barrel of the gun and aimed at Jones's feet.

The gunshot made a louder noise than any of them expected. The bullet tore a piece of bone and flesh from Jones's ankle, forcing him to drop heavily to the floor.

"Now, both of you get the fuck over there! And lay down on the floor! Lay down with your hands straight out, or there's another shot coming!"

Jones managed to raise himself up but with a bloody and painfully damaged ankle. He limped on one foot into the center of the living room where he joined his shaken partner, Mr. Pratt.

Andy was in total shock at what had just happened. He couldn't believe he just shot another human being. But he remained quietly confident, keeping the barrel of the pistol aimed on the two men.

Just then, the sound of police sirens blared outside of the cabin. Cruisers came rolling up onto the property followed by shouting and screaming coming from the SWAT team.

Within minutes, the officers stormed into the isolated cabin with drawn guns. They quickly sorted out the potentially dangerous confrontation. They took the government-issued gun from Andy's hand then swiftly handcuffed the two men lying face down on the floor. One of the cops read them the Miranda Act then ushered them outside and into a cruiser.

A team of EMTs ran into the bedroom to evaluate Miss Lakely. The teacher was next seen with an oxygen mask on her face while being wheeled out of the cabin on a gurney. The first responders rushed her into an ambulance destined for the hospital emergency room.

After some initial questioning, an officer escorted Becky, Andy, and Amber into a police cruiser and sped off to the local police station.

Inside the old fashioned brick and mortar precinct, a detective led them into a conference room and offered them cold drinks. They now had to give a detailed incident report to the law enforcement authorities.

But before they did this, they each called their parents, providing them with a brief explanation of what had happened after that first night on Hook Island. They would fill in the details after their parents came to pick them up.

CHAPTER TWENTY-TWO

The FBI worked swiftly with state and local police to pressure the arrested Mr. Pratt. Since he was destined for a long prison conviction, he cooperated in exchange for a more lenient sentence in a white-collar penitentiary.

The high school principal explained to the authorities how he and Barry Jones set up the underground lab operation, combining his money and the former teacher's chemistry expertise. He further disclosed how he had learned later that Jones had drugged and raped Cindy Shea. He told them how the creepy Chemistry teacher panicked that she might remember him that fateful night. The disturbed teacher had set her up in a manipulated and lethal car accident. He put the drugged young woman into the driver's seat before pushing her car over the side of the steep hillside road.

In addition to making a large sum of drug money, the pervert's motivation was to have sex with young girls. According to Pratt, Jones argued he needed to test out the new formula of drug-rape pills. The retiring principal confessed his own interest was purely financial and he wanted to do this for only the short term.

Pratt admitted he had arranged and facilitated Jones's sexual assault on Amber Woods during that April vacation afternoon in the Bantam Lake cabin. He had lured her up to the remote cabin for Jones's perverted sexual bonus. He also confessed that Jones had murdered Jack, the FBI informant. The two had an argument out on Hook Island very late one night. Jack was upset over the Cindy Shea rape and murder. The confrontation got nasty outside and Jones shot Jack at close range using his own nine-millimeter handgun. Later, when convenient, and with Pratt's help, they dumped Jack's body into Peck's Pond.

For days, the news of the recent crimes buzzed in the quiet, middle-class, bedroom town of North Haven, Connecticut.

Pratt's nephew, Nate Simpson, was arrested for complicity in the crimes and would be tried and sentenced separately.

Barry Jones was destined for a quick conviction and life without parole in a maximum security penitentiary.

The murders and drug lab linked to the school principal and former teacher were like no other story in the history of the colonial town.

Becky Bing and Andy Abbot were publicly credited with assisting the FBI, but no details were ever revealed to protect their under-aged status.

* * *

A week later, the local media cooled down and life slowly returned to its normal routine for Becky and Andy.

But they met privately one last time with Miss Lakely, aka FBI agent, Amanda White, for lunch at a New Haven restaurant. The meeting was strangely both somber and uplifting.

Amanda would soon move on, never to return to the Connecticut area. She told the two teens how she'd be forever grateful to them for saving her life when she was incapacitated with the date-rape drugs.

At the luncheon, she told the two best friends how the FBI arranged for a special certified citation and an official award from headquarters in Washington, D.C. to be given to them. It was a tearful goodbye with warm hugs before they left the restaurant.

With Amanda's departure, there would be a new homeroom teacher in Room 205 once again this coming fall.

On the walk home, Becky and Andy reflected on their beloved teacher.

"I'm really gonna miss her. I liked her a lot!" Andy commented.

"Yeah, I will too, but for different reasons than those that you and all the other boys have! If she wasn't such a hot-looking chick, you guys would think of her as just another teacher. And Andy, you surprise me! I happen to remember you telling me that you wished you had never taken the AP Logic class. You told me you had really wanted to take another advanced math course."

The tall, young man chuckled.

"No, not really. But Becky, that's not why I really liked Miss Lakely. I just thought she was cool and taught us a lot about the basic points of Logic. Especially the one about—we should never ASSUME. You know, like the assumption you just made why you thought I liked our teacher."

Becky turned to her boyfriend and stuck her tongue out at him. It was payback time for her from when she caught him in the same pitfall some weeks ago. He laughed at her mock childish reaction.

A week later, on a hot, late August afternoon, the two strolled slowly once again hand in hand toward Wollaston Beach. Each carried a beach bag filled with the requisite snacks, towels, iPods, and suntan lotion.

Their friend, Bumper Stone, who had finally returned from New York City, caught up with them as he pedaled his bike. His thick, chubby legs slowly churned to maintain the casual pace with the strolling couple.

"Hey, Bump, what's up?"

"Not much since I just talked with you last night. But, I gotta tell ya, you guys made a helluva name for yourselves," he said. "Geez, I'm only gone for a short time and the whole town goes freakin' nuts. I mean, murder, rape, drugs! And, now you two are heroes for saving Miss Lakely and solving the crime! And I thought I was having the coolest time in New York City doing some crazy things. Now I feel like I was in a kiddie sandbox compared to what you guys uncovered back here in Beechwood Knoll!"

Becky looked obliquely at the husky friend who pedaled alongside.

"Yeah, Bumper, and if it weren't for you and your nutty idea to get a vid of a 'wannabe' rock band, this never would have happened. And because of that crazy plan and what happened, I'll never step foot onto Hook Island for the rest of my life!"

"Well, I'm glad I could oblige you," he replied, with a mock sarcasm. "And on top if it all, I find out that you guys have a love thing goin' on. Geez, I tell you, this has been one crazy, freakin' summer. I guess I better stick around for a while to make sure things settle back to normal again."

They all grinned at the comment. Andy turned to Bumper.

"Hey, Bump, why don't you ride ahead of us? I need to show Becky something that's not too far from here. And…it's kinda personal. We'll catch up with you at the beach in a few minutes. Save a blanket spot for us."

"Huh? Oh yeah, sure. I want to get down there anyways and take a cool dip. I missed the ocean while I was down in the city."

Bumper accelerated his bike pedaling and soon was fifty yards in front of them.

"So, Andy, what is it you needed to show me?" Becky asked.

"Oh, it's just a little something. And it's personal and private…I mean, private and personal just for you and me."

"Is it something about your now becoming a man with the courage you showed out at Bantam Lake?"

"Hmm. Well, I am proud of what I did out there. Especially, since I never shot a gun before in my life. Hell, I never even held one before."

"But you did become brave in that single instant."

"Yeah, but that's not becoming a man….at least from what I've been told. I'm still not a man…technically."

Becky stopped walking and turned to face him.

"Andy, you are a man! And that goes for technically becoming a man, too!"

His hand went down to her chin then gently lifted up her head. Then he leaned into her and gave her a soft kiss on the lips.

"Hey, it's at the next corner. C'mon, I want to see your reaction."

When they reached the now infamous corner of Bridge Street leading out to the bridge to Hook Island, Becky stopped dead in her tracks.

"Oh, no! You're not getting me to cross over that bridge again. My days and nights spent over at that hell-hole are only memories and I have no intentions of returning to Hook Island!"

"No, no. I don't want you to cross over the bridge. I just want you to look up at that big, old elm tree right in front of us."

Becky looked at the centuries-old magnificent tree. The impressive spreading branches provided a cooling shade from the hot August sun.

"Yeah, it's nice. I love trees, but what's so special about this one?"

"Look up at that knife carving up there."

Becky raised her head and spotted freshly carved letters in the tree's bark. The newly made marking was on a huge limb stretching out over the road.

"But what is that? What does it mean?"

"It's algebra, Beck. You're good at mathematics, like me."

"Yeah, I am pretty good at algebra, but those letters or rather that formula doesn't make any sense. It looks like—$A^2 + B^2 = \infty$. But I would think it should be the standard Pythagorean Theorem. You know, $A^2 + B^2 = C^2$. I haven't a clue what that carved-out algebraic expression means. I've never seen any formula like that before."

"Well, think about it and break it down. What's another way to express A^2?" Andy asked.

"Oh, well, that's A squared. It's equal to A times A, or algebraically it's just AA."

"Right. And…how about B^2?"

"That's the same thing. It's B squared and is equal to B times B or, just BB."

"Good! Now what does the symbol '∞' mean?"

"That's the mathematic symbol or scientific notation for infinity. It means, forever."

"Okay, so now say out loud the algebra expression in the way you just translated it."

"AA and BB forever!" she said.

"You got it, Becky. See, that's our secret love formula. I knew you'd get it. It means Andy Abbot and Becky Bing forever! And nobody who ever walks by this old elm tree will know our secret formula carved into that old tree; just you and me."

Becky giggled for several moments. She then got up on her tiptoes and faced her taller friend, looking into his eyes. She grabbed his shoulders and kissed him warmly on his lips.

"Andy, you're such a romantic! You're a freakin' nerd, but you're my romantic nerd."

The two giggled in unison as they continued their walk, hand in hand.

This summer season and all that it had brought to them was closing a chapter of their young lives. And now there would be time to enjoy living—simply as teenagers. But they would never forget what they experienced during this special summer of Hook Island.

ABOUT THE AUTHOR

Gordon Mathieson has been writing fiction professionally for over ten years. Prior to that, he published articles in his careers as both a Chinese translator and later as Director of Computing at Yale University.

His other published titles are:

QUISSET

THE HYANNIS HOUSE

THE GREATER BOSTON CHALLENGE

THE COLOR of ICE

He now lives on Cape Cod, Massachusetts.

Hook Island is the first in his series of Becky Bing mystery novels.

The sequel will be released soon.

Visit Gordon online at www.gordonmathieson.com

Made in the USA
San Bernardino, CA
29 August 2014